- HERGÉ -
★

THE ADVENTURES OF TINTIN

THE SECRET
OF THE UNICORN

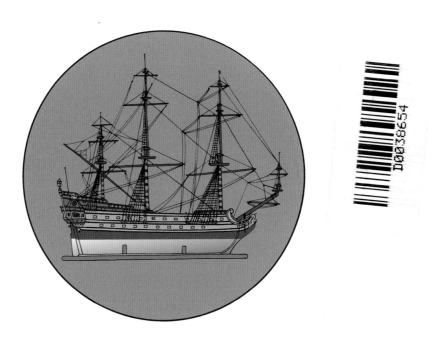

Little, Brown and Company
New York   Boston

www.casterman.com
www.tintin.com

Little, Brown and Company
Hachette Book Group
237 Park Avenue, New York, NY 10017
Visit our website at www.lb-kids.com

First Edition: May 2011

ISBN: 978-0-316-13386-9
2011921034
SC
Printed in China

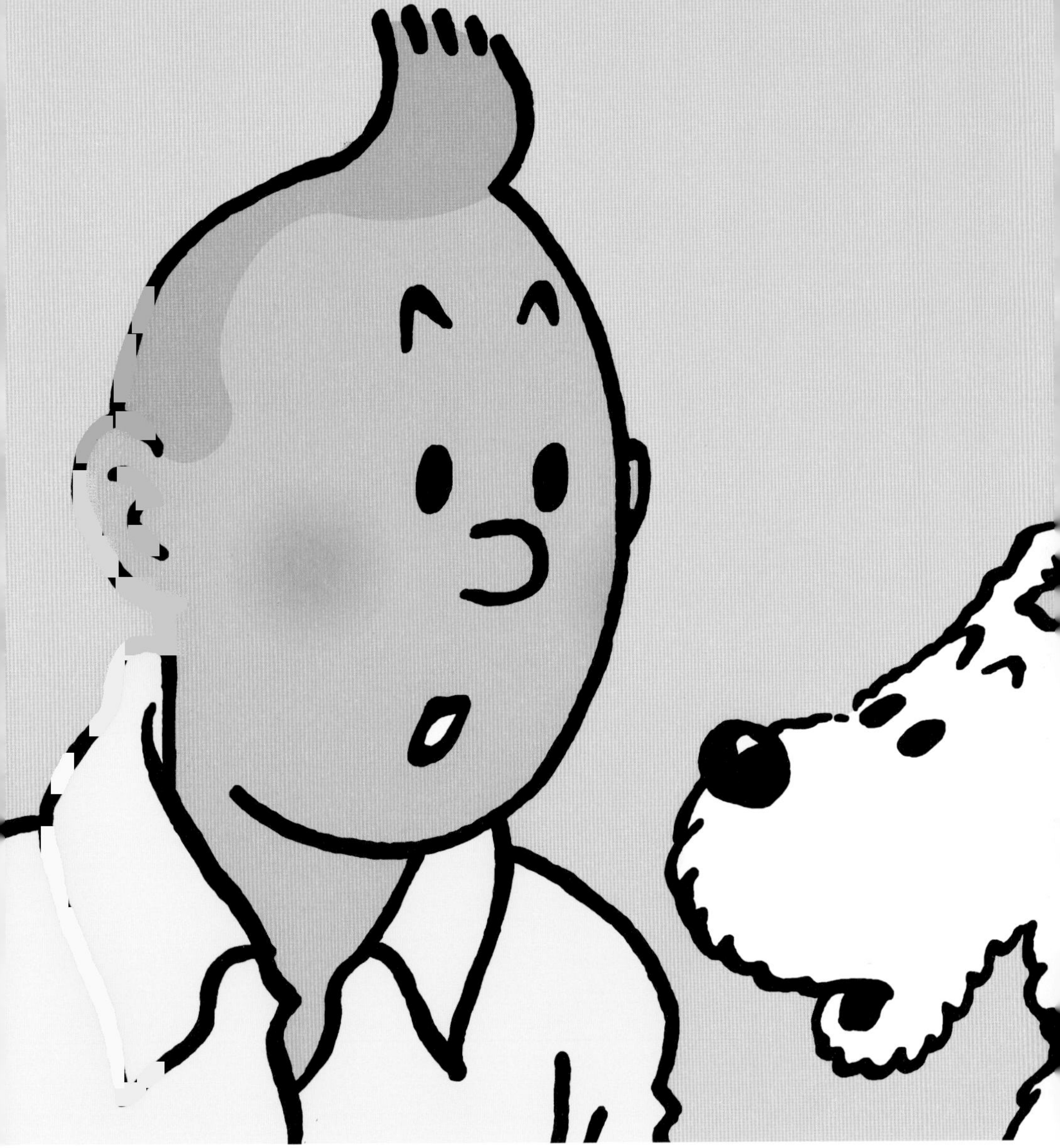

Tintin and Snowy

Tintin is a brave young reporter
who loves to solve mysteries and fight crime!
Tintin's faithful dog, Snowy,
follows his master wherever he goes.

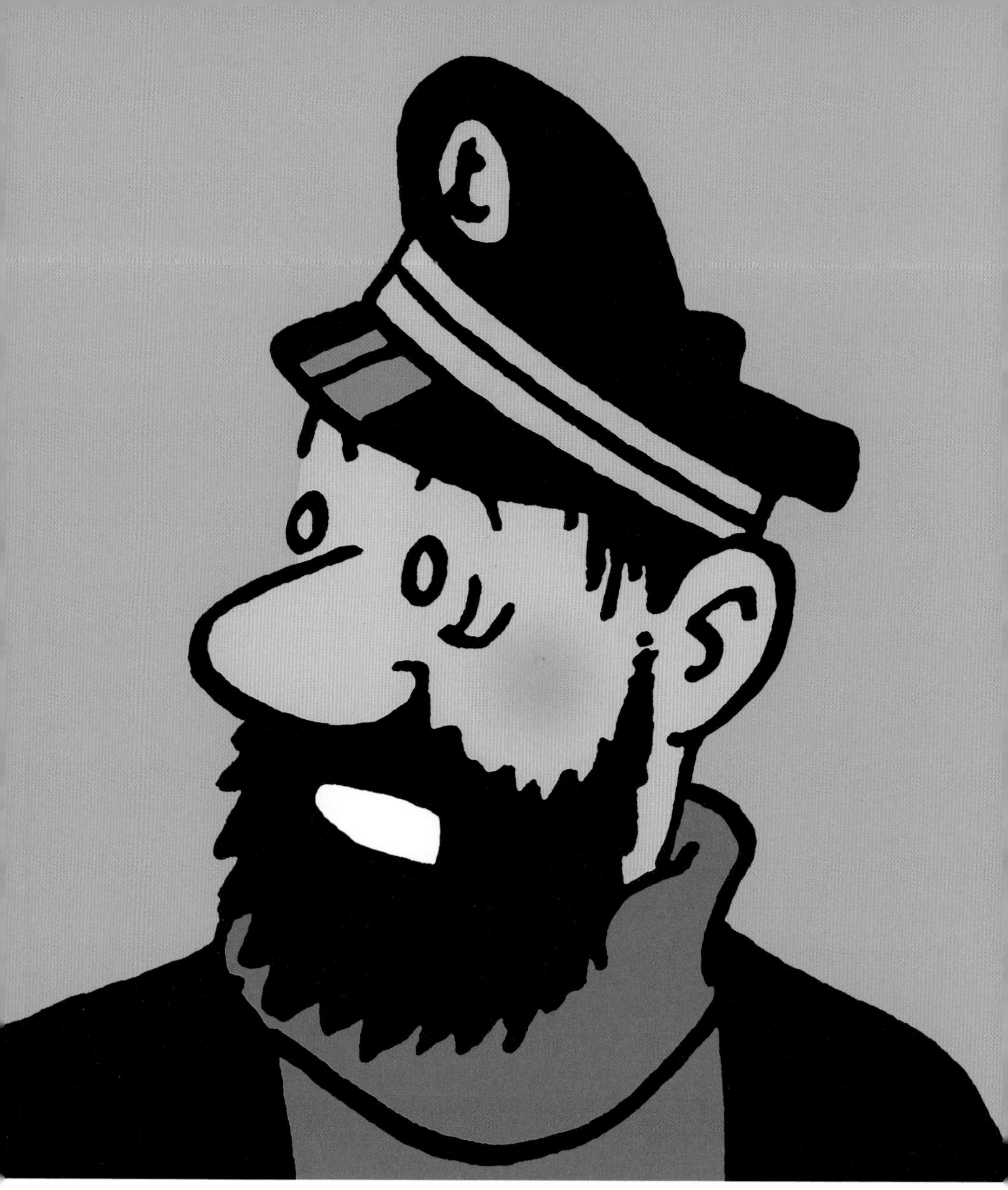

Captain Haddock

Tintin's best friend. Although quick to anger,
the captain has a heart of gold and would lay down his life
for his young companion.

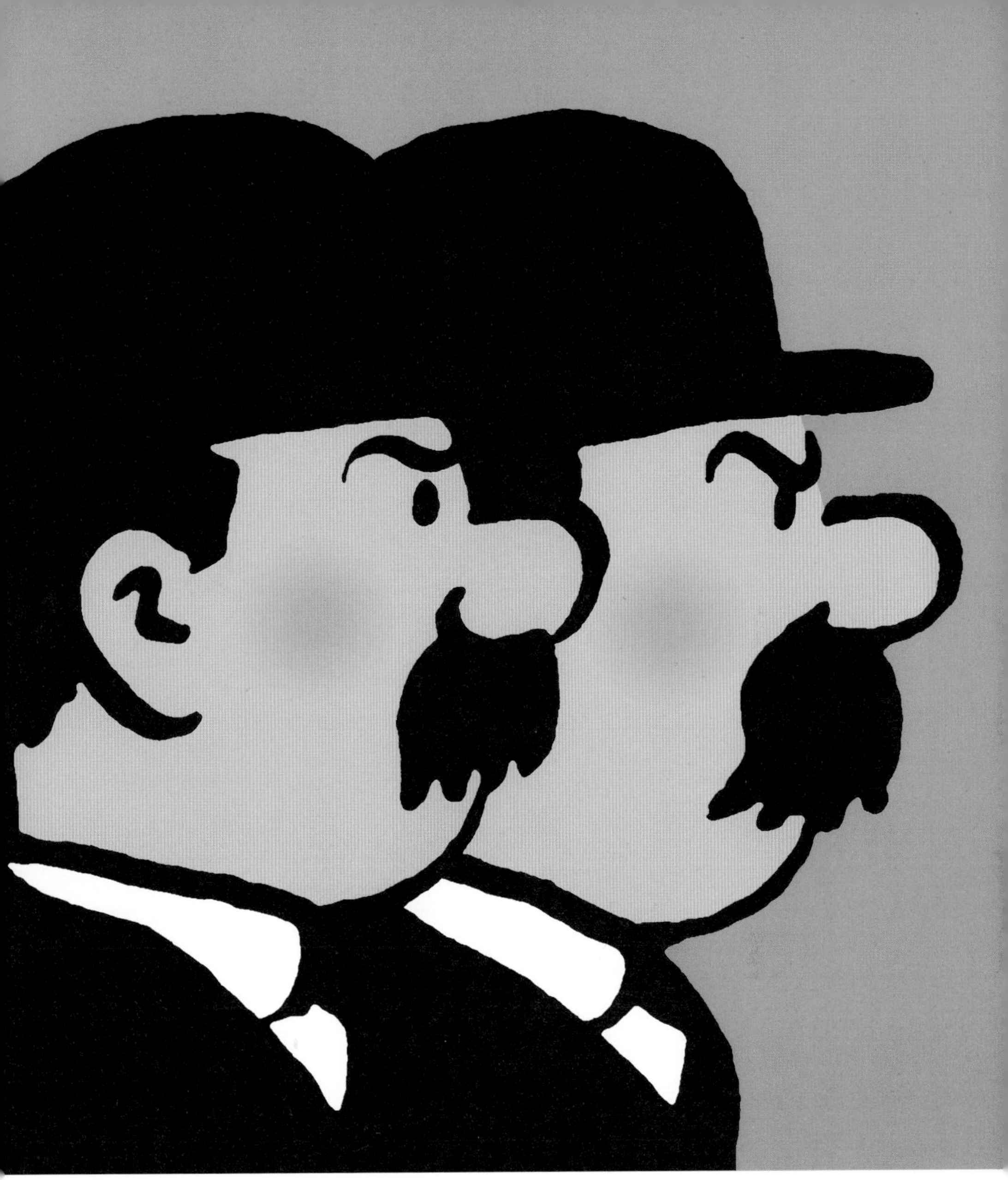

Thomson and Thompson

As stubborn as they are similar, the Thom(p)sons are a pair of bumbling police detectives who are determined to enforce the law. . . at all costs!

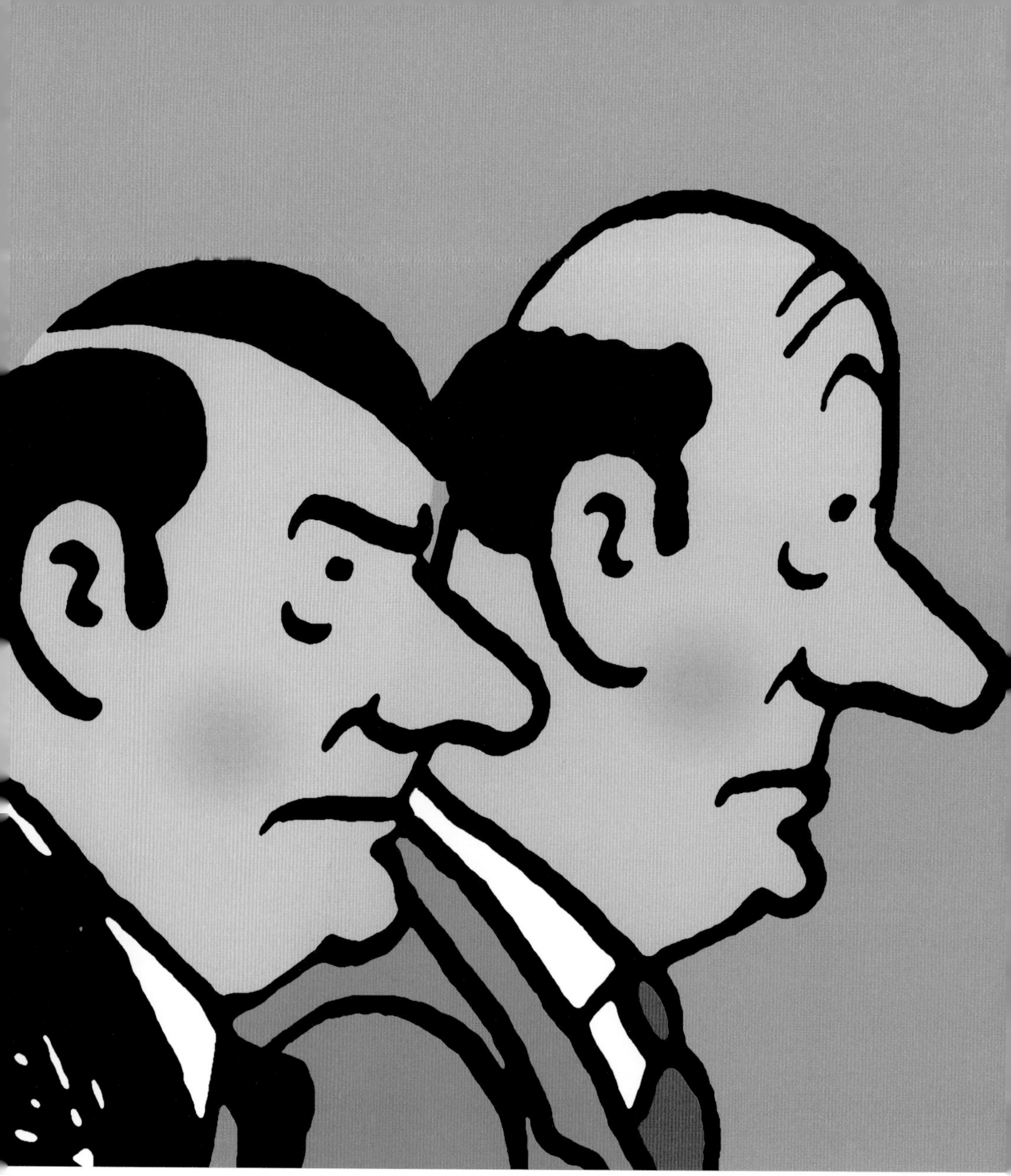

The Bird brothers

Greedy antique dealers, the Bird brothers won't let anything or anyone get in their way. They are highly dangerous criminals.

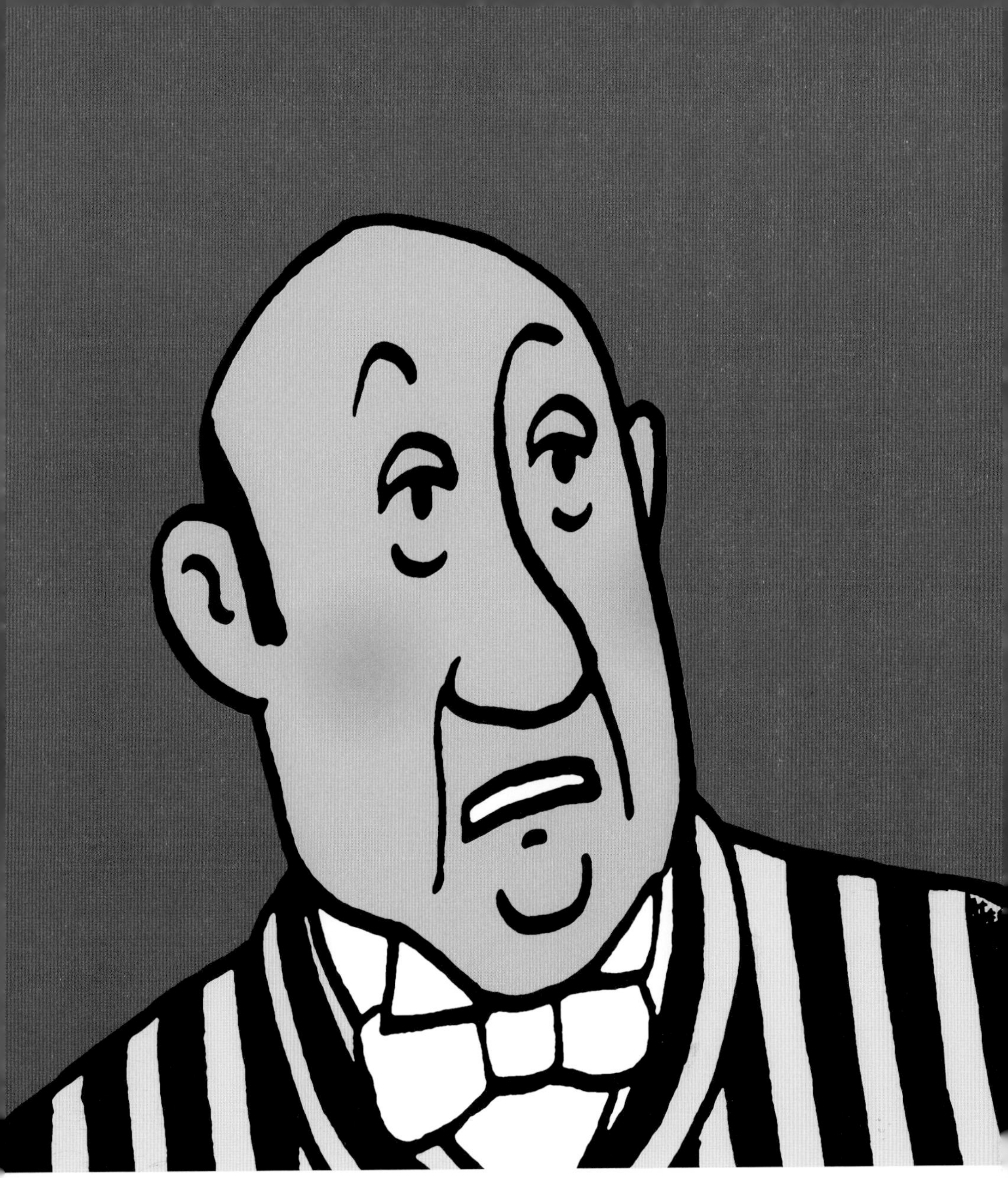

Nestor

The dependable and loyal servant at Marlinspike Hall.
The only problem with Nestor is his employers!

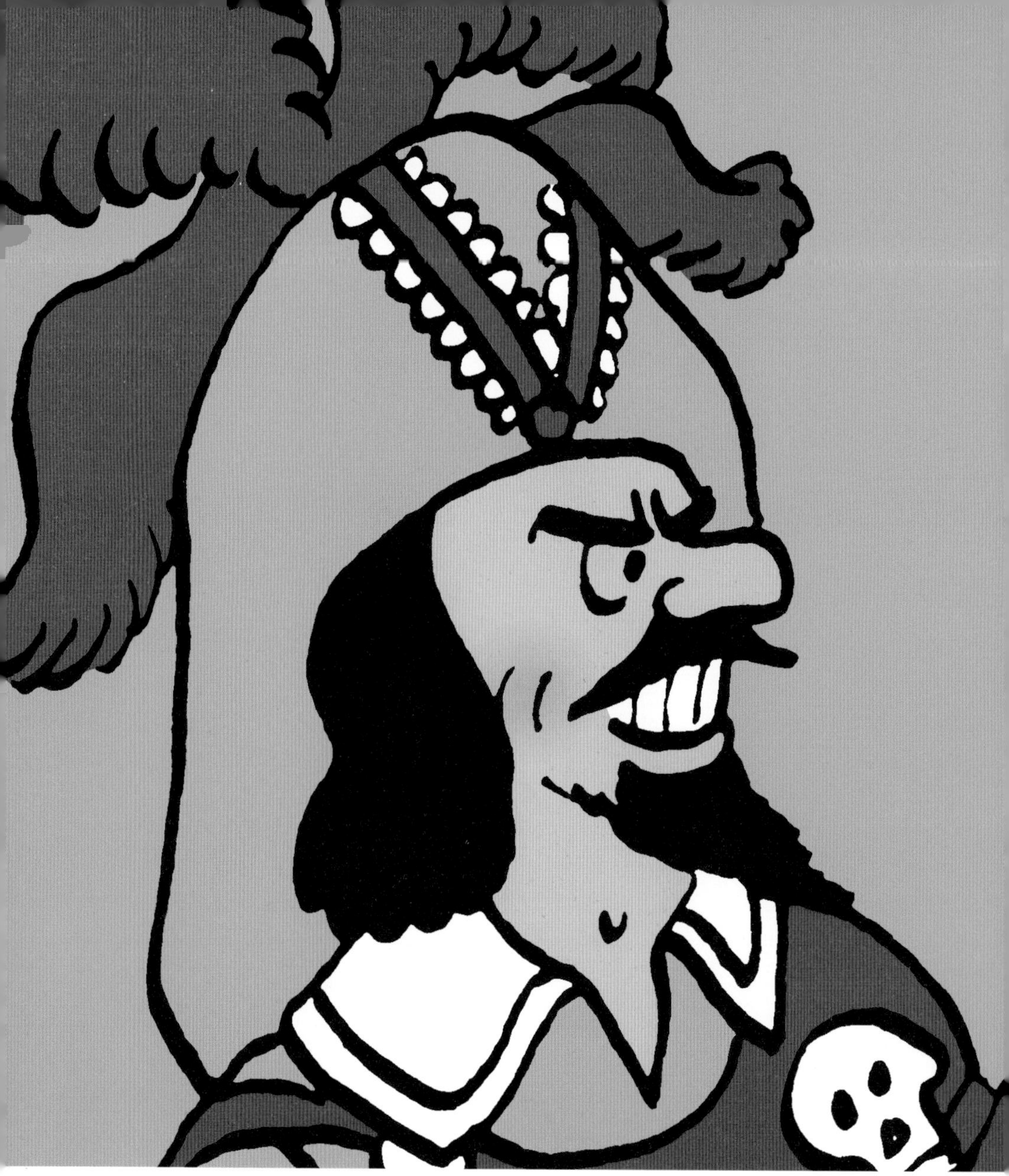

Red Rackham

Red Rackham was a ruthless and bloodthirsty pirate who lived over 300 years ago.

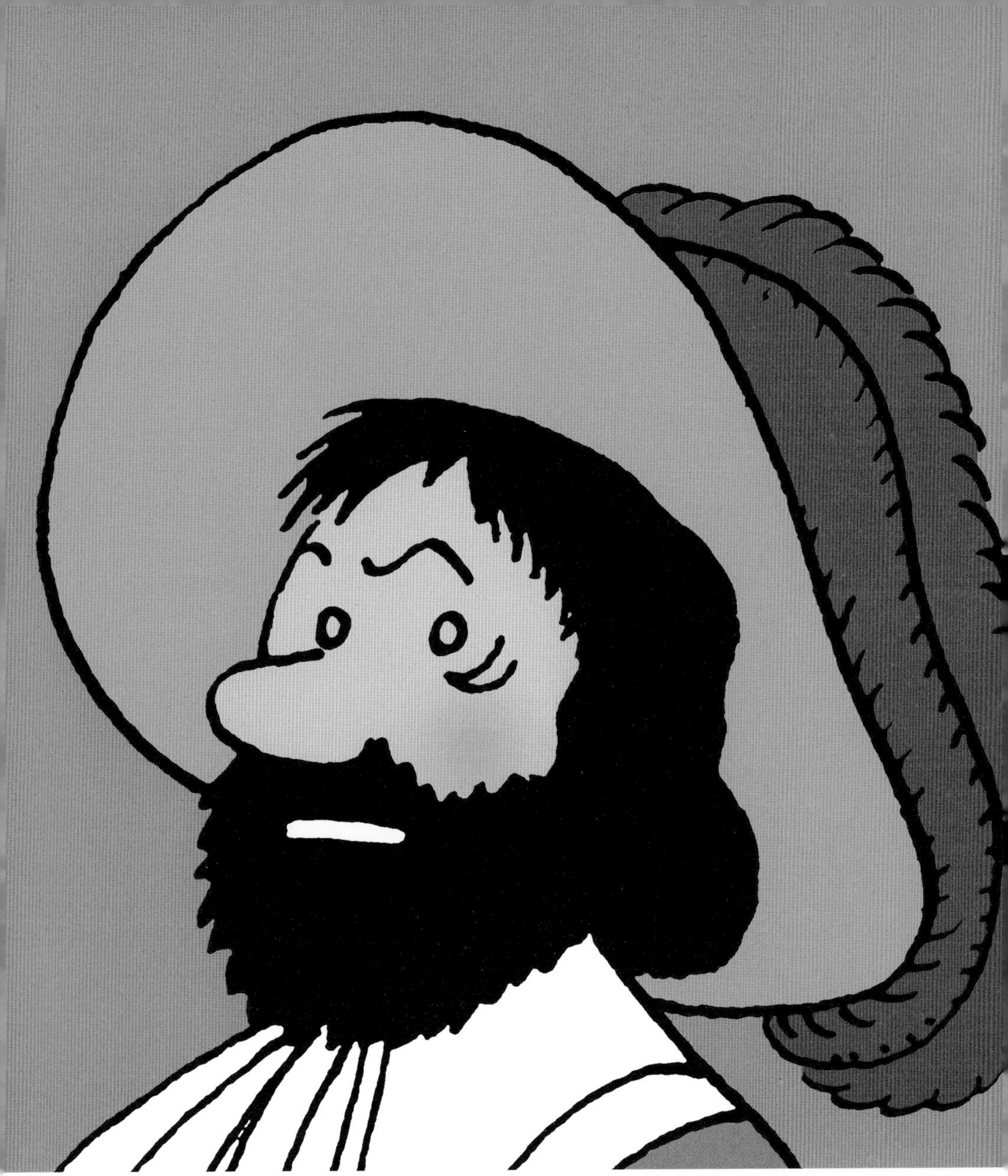

Sir Francis Haddock

Captain Haddock's brave ancestor.
Sir Francis Haddock was the Commander of the *Unicorn*
and the archenemy of Red Rackham.

THE SECRET OF *THE UNICORN*

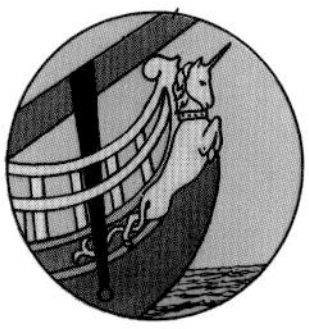

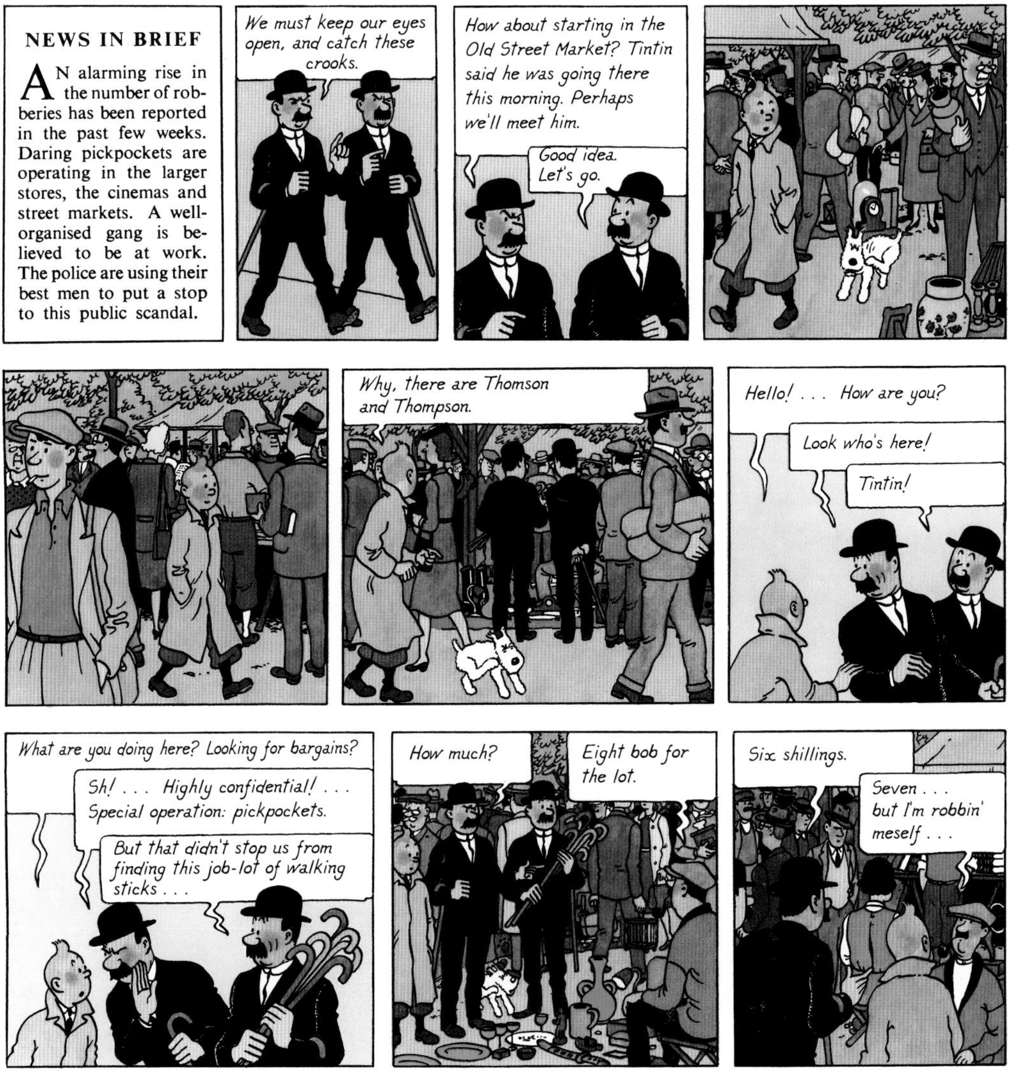
NEWS IN BRIEF
AN alarming rise in the number of robberies has been reported in the past few weeks. Daring pickpockets are operating in the larger stores, the cinemas and street markets. A well-organised gang is believed to be at work. The police are using their best men to put a stop to this public scandal.
We must keep our eyes open, and catch these crooks.
How about starting in the Old Street Market? Tintin said he was going there this morning. Perhaps we'll meet him.
Good idea. Let's go.
Why, there are Thomson and Thompson.
Hello! . . . How are you?
Look who's here!
Tintin!
What are you doing here? Looking for bargains?
Sh! . . . Highly confidential! . . . Special operation: pickpockets.
But that didn't stop us from finding this job-lot of walking sticks . . .
How much?
Eight bob for the lot.
Six shillings.
Seven . . . but I'm robbin' meself . . .

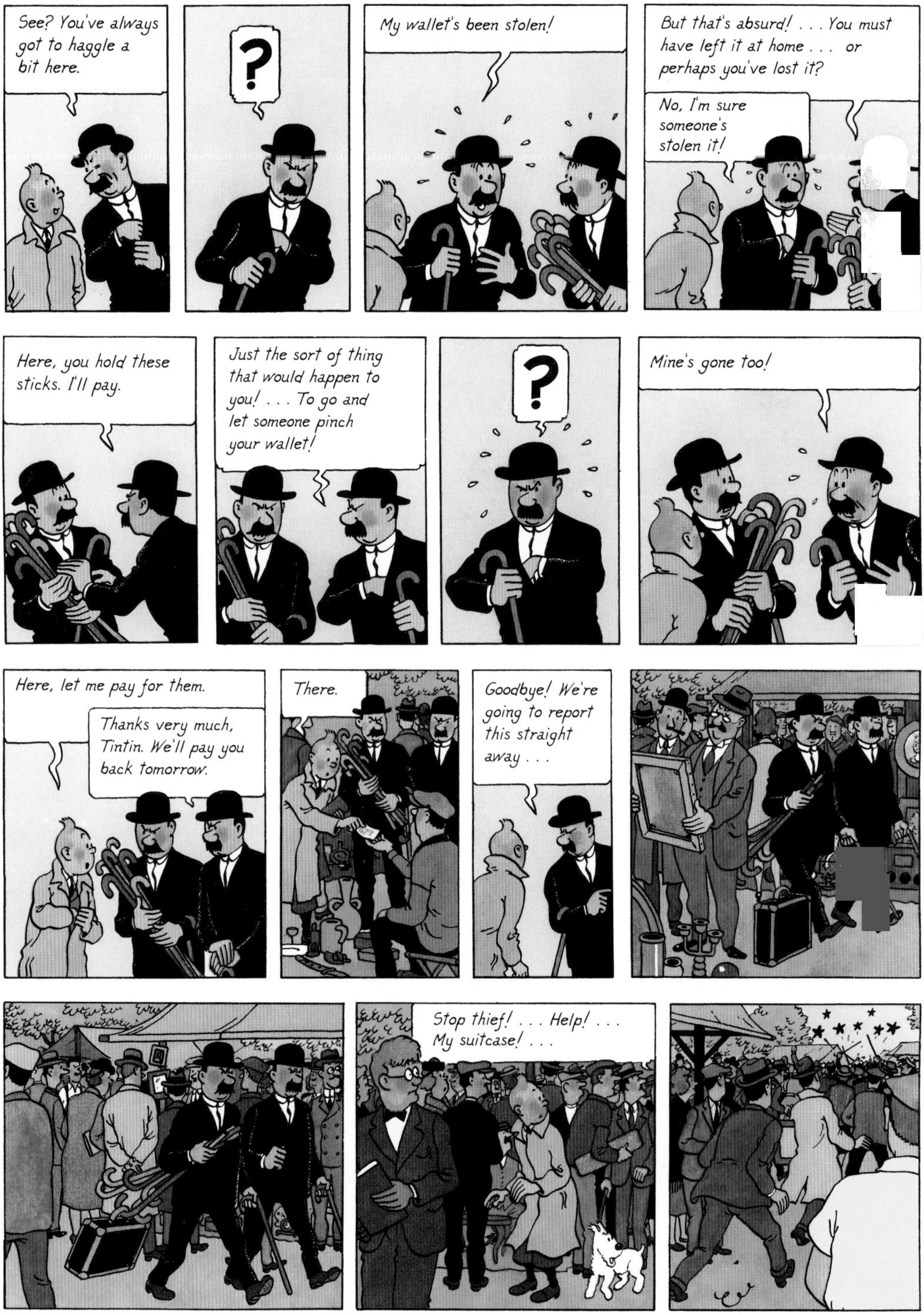
See? You've always got to haggle a bit here.
?
My wallet's been stolen!
But that's absurd! . . . You must have left it at home . . . or perhaps you've lost it?
No, I'm sure someone's stolen it!
Here, you hold these sticks. I'll pay.
Just the sort of thing that would happen to you! . . . To go and let someone pinch your wallet!
?
Mine's gone too!
Here, let me pay for them.
Thanks very much, Tintin. We'll pay you back tomorrow.
There.
Goodbye! We're going to report this straight away . . .
Stop thief! . . . Help! . . . My suitcase! . . .

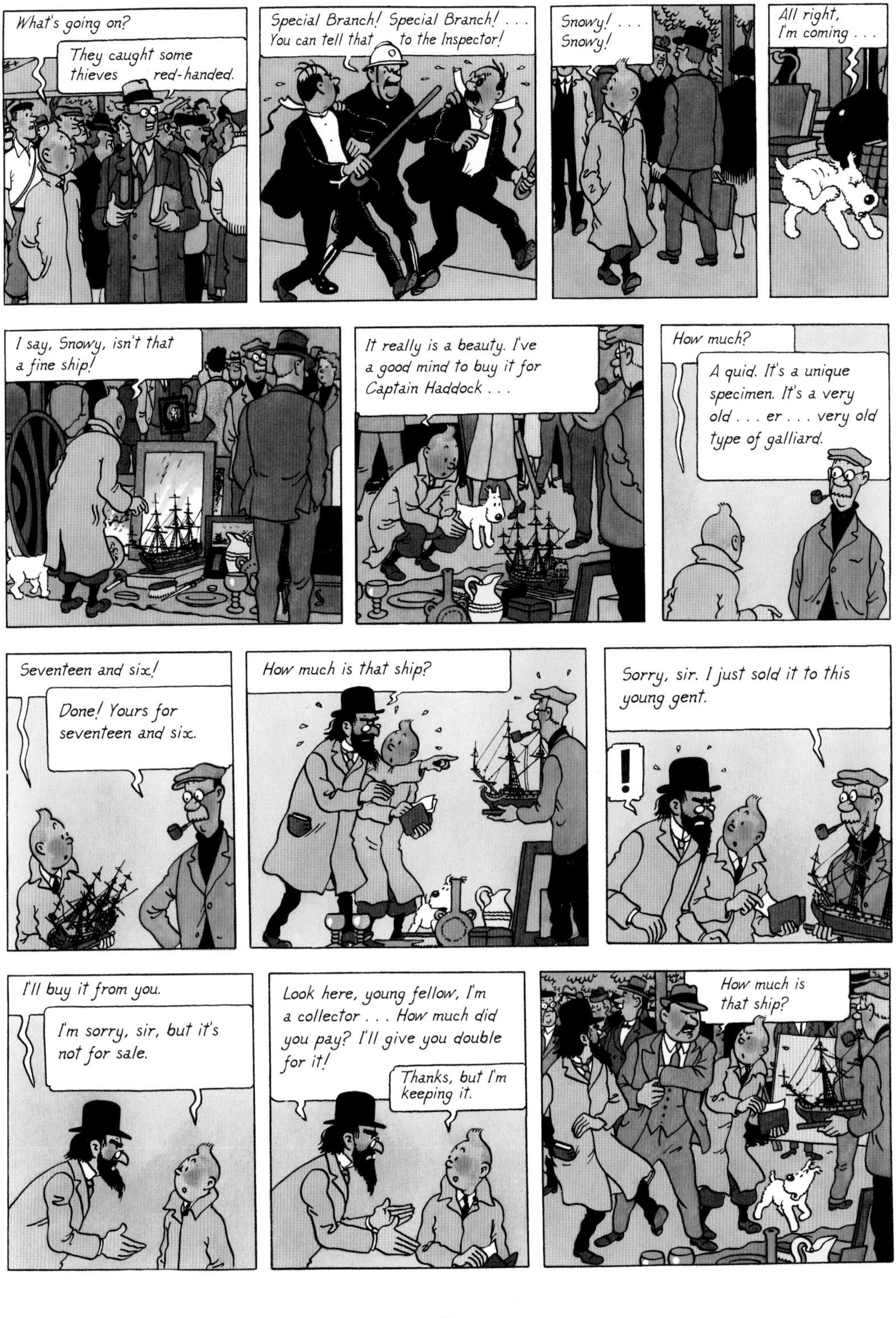

What's going on?
They caught some thieves red-handed.
Special Branch! Special Branch! . . . You can tell that to the Inspector!
Snowy! . . . Snowy!
All right, I'm coming . . .
I say, Snowy, isn't that a fine ship!
It really is a beauty. I've a good mind to buy it for Captain Haddock . . .
How much?
A quid. It's a unique specimen. It's a very old . . . er . . . very old type of galliard.
Seventeen and six!
Done! Yours for seventeen and six.
How much is that ship?
Sorry, sir. I just sold it to this young gent.
!
I'll buy it from you.
I'm sorry, sir, but it's not for sale.
Look here, young fellow, I'm a collector . . . How much did you pay? I'll give you double for it!
Thanks, but I'm keeping it.
How much is that ship?

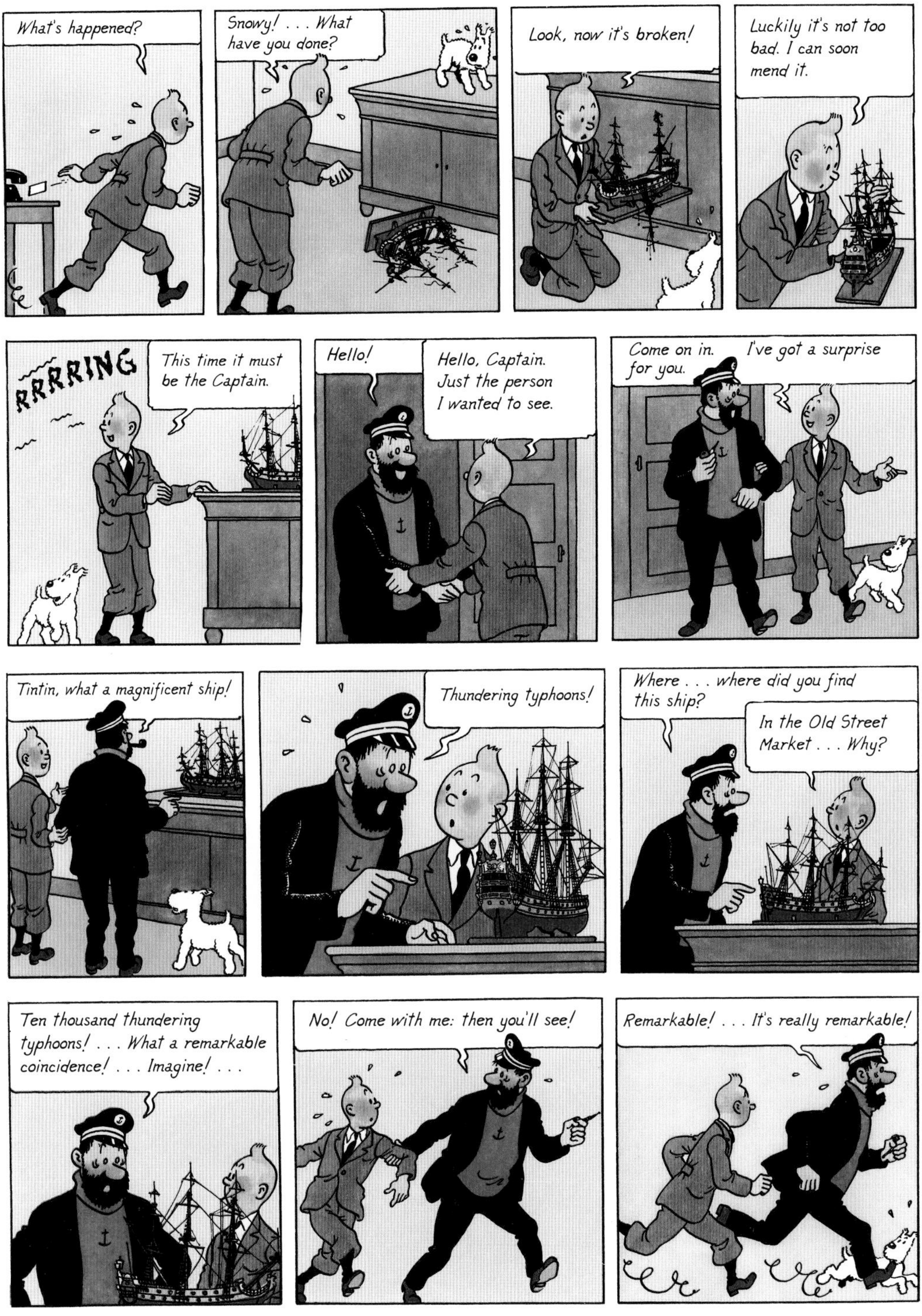
What's happened?
Snowy! . . . What have you done?
Look, now it's broken!
Luckily it's not too bad. I can soon mend it.
RRRRING
This time it must be the Captain.
Hello!
Hello, Captain. Just the person I wanted to see.
Come on in. I've got a surprise for you.
Tintin, what a magnificent ship!
Thundering typhoons!
Where . . . where did you find this ship?
In the Old Street Market . . . Why?
Ten thousand thundering typhoons! . . . What a remarkable coincidence! . . . Imagine! . . .
No! Come with me: then you'll see!
Remarkable! . . . It's really remarkable!

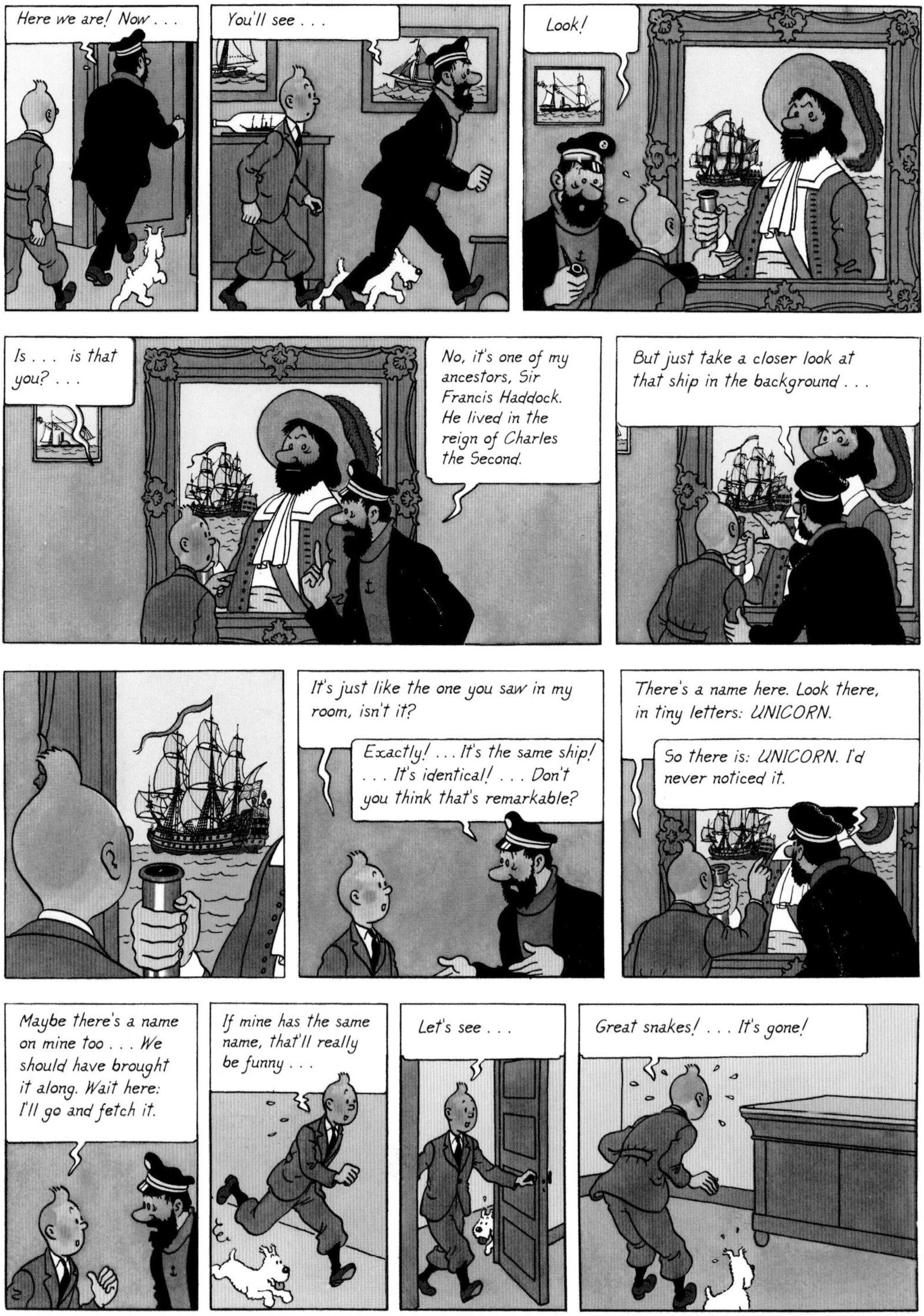

Here we are! Now . . .
You'll see . . .
Look!
Is . . . is that you? . . .
No, it's one of my ancestors, Sir Francis Haddock. He lived in the reign of Charles the Second.
But just take a closer look at that ship in the background . . .
It's just like the one you saw in my room, isn't it?
Exactly! . . . It's the same ship! . . . It's identical! . . . Don't you think that's remarkable?
There's a name here. Look there, in tiny letters: UNICORN.
So there is: UNICORN. I'd never noticed it.
Maybe there's a name on mine too . . . We should have brought it along. Wait here: I'll go and fetch it.
If mine has the same name, that'll really be funny . . .
Let's see . . .
Great snakes! . . . It's gone!

RRRING...
RRRING...
RRRING...

Hello? . . . Yes . . . Ah, it's you . . . Well, has your ship got the same name? . . . What did you say? . . . It's been stolen?

Yes, stolen! . . . Do I suspect anybody? No one at all . . . at least . . . Look Captain, I'll ring you again later . . .

Yes . . . he's the only possibility . . .

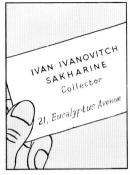

IVAN IVANOVITCH
SAKHARINE
Collector

21, Eucalyptus Avenue

Just you wait, Mr Ivan Ivanovitch Sakharine!

Here we are . . .

EUCALYPTUS AVENUE

I've a hunch that we're off on one of our adventures again . . .

RRRING

21

Something tells me he's going to get a surprise when he opens the door!

Ah, there you are! . . . Come in . . . I was expecting you.

!

What? . . . Expecting me? . . . Then you know why I've come.

But of course . . .

You've come to tell me that you'll sell your ship after all . . .

Certainly not!

No? . . . Then I don't understand . . .

Is this where you keep your collection? . . . I've come to tell you, sir . . . that my ship has been stolen . . .

. . . and that I'm waiting for you to explain how it comes to be here!

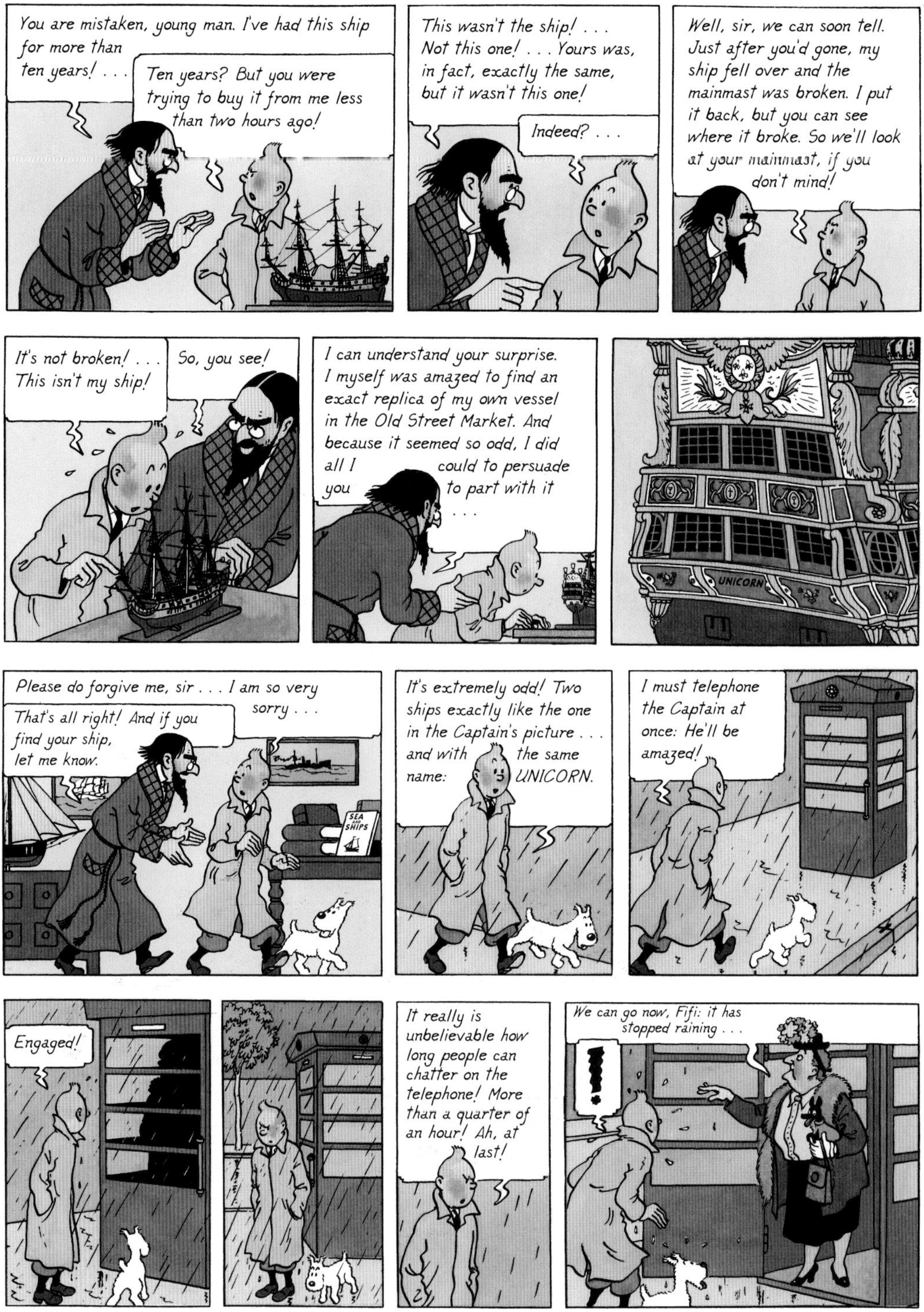

You are mistaken, young man. I've had this ship for more than ten years! . . .
Ten years? But you were trying to buy it from me less than two hours ago!
This wasn't the ship! . . . Not this one! . . . Yours was, in fact, exactly the same, but it wasn't this one!
Indeed? . . .
Well, sir, we can soon tell. Just after you'd gone, my ship fell over and the mainmast was broken. I put it back, but you can see where it broke. So we'll look at your mainmast, if you don't mind!
It's not broken! . . . This isn't my ship!
So, you see!
I can understand your surprise. I myself was amazed to find an exact replica of my own vessel in the Old Street Market. And because it seemed so odd, I did all I could to persuade you to part with it . . .
UNICORN
Please do forgive me, sir . . . I am so very sorry . . .
That's all right! And if you find your ship, let me know.
SEA AND SHIPS
It's extremely odd! Two ships exactly like the one in the Captain's picture . . . and with the same name: UNICORN.
I must telephone the Captain at once: He'll be amazed!
Engaged!
It really is unbelievable how long people can chatter on the telephone! More than a quarter of an hour! Ah, at last!
We can go now, Fifi: it has stopped raining . . .

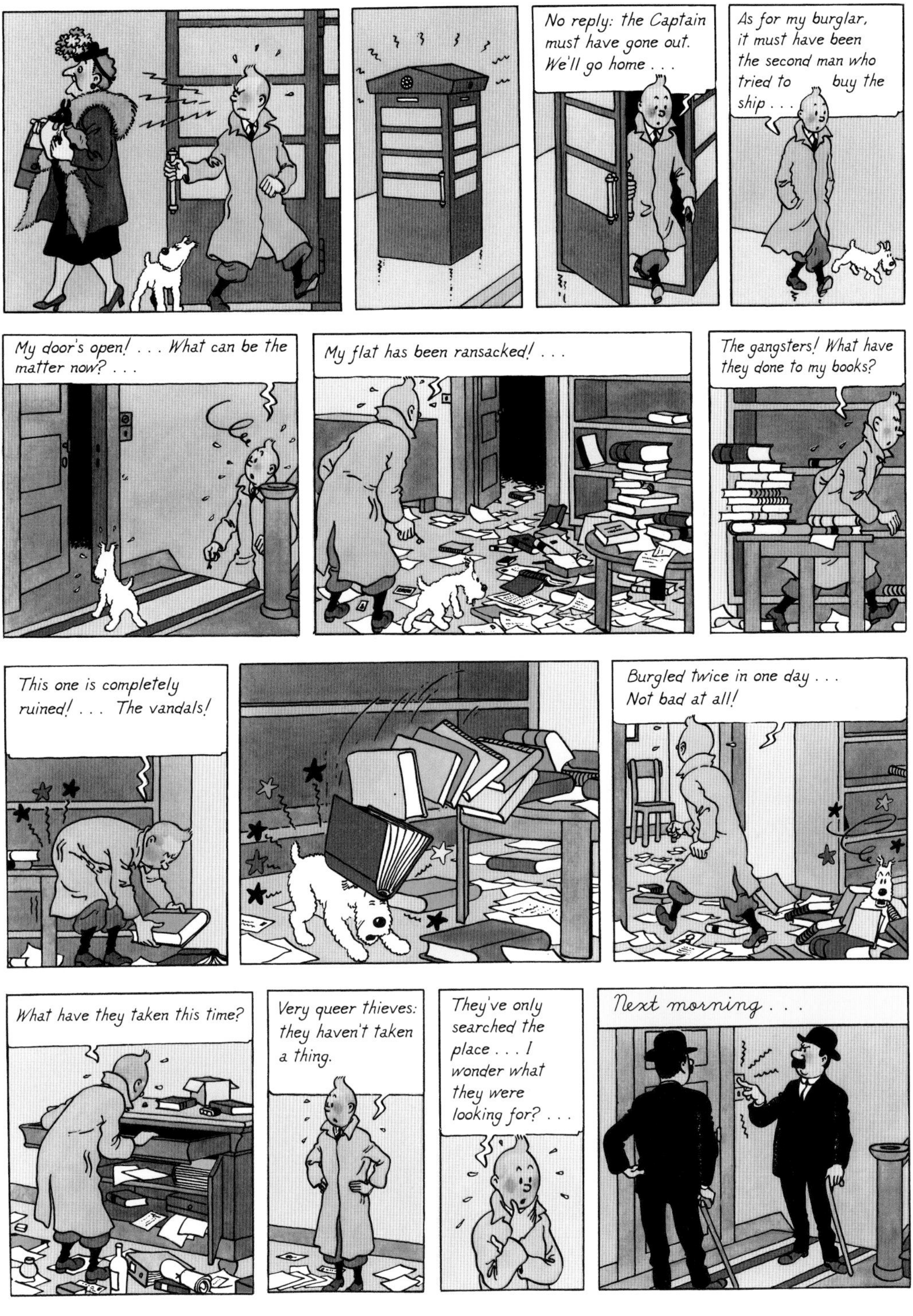
No reply: the Captain must have gone out. We'll go home . . .
As for my burglar, it must have been the second man who tried to buy the ship . . .
My door's open! . . . What can be the matter now? . . .
My flat has been ransacked! . . .
The gangsters! What have they done to my books?
This one is completely ruined! . . . The vandals!
Burgled twice in one day . . . Not bad at all!
What have they taken this time?
Very queer thieves: they haven't taken a thing.
They've only searched the place . . . I wonder what they were looking for? . . .
Next morning . . .

Hello. How are you? . . . Good heavens! Whatever's happened?

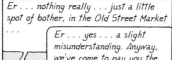

Er . . . nothing really . . . just a little spot of bother, in the Old Street Market . . .

Er . . . yes . . . a slight misunderstanding. Anyway, we've come to pay you the money for those sticks. We called last night, but you were out.

Did you get your wallet back all right?

I'm afraid not. But I bought a new one this morning, and . . . and . . .

Goodness gracious! I've been robbed again!

Great Scotland Yard! . . . That man we met last night on the stairs on our way here! . . . I remember now: he bumped into me! . . .

What was he like?

He bumped into me, too!

Quite tall . . . coarse features . . . black hair . . . small black moustache . . . blue suit . . . brown hat . . .

That's him . . . the man from the Old Street Market!

But he couldn't have stolen your wallet last night, when you only bought it this morning.

There's something in what you say . . .

Miserable thieves! A brand new wallet! Come along, Thomson, we must report this right away!

He's right! . . . We must report it at once . . .

Look out!

Hey, Thompson, wait for me. Where are you? . . .

Here! . . . I'm downstairs already!

Poor old Thomsons, they do have rotten luck! . . . There seems to be quite an epidemic of larceny and house-breaking.

Oh well, let's try and get these papers sorted out . . .

What are you after, Snowy?

A cigarette, under there? That's a funny place . . .

Why, it's not a cigarette . . . it's a little scroll of parchment . . .

But this isn't mine! Where ever did it come from? . . . Let's have a closer look at it . . .

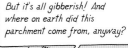

Here's another mystery!

But it's all gibberish! And where on earth did this parchment come from, anyway?

Three Brothers joyned. Three Vnicornes in company sailing in the noonday Sunne will speak. For 'tis from the Light that Light will dawn. And then shines forth the Eagle's

42

1

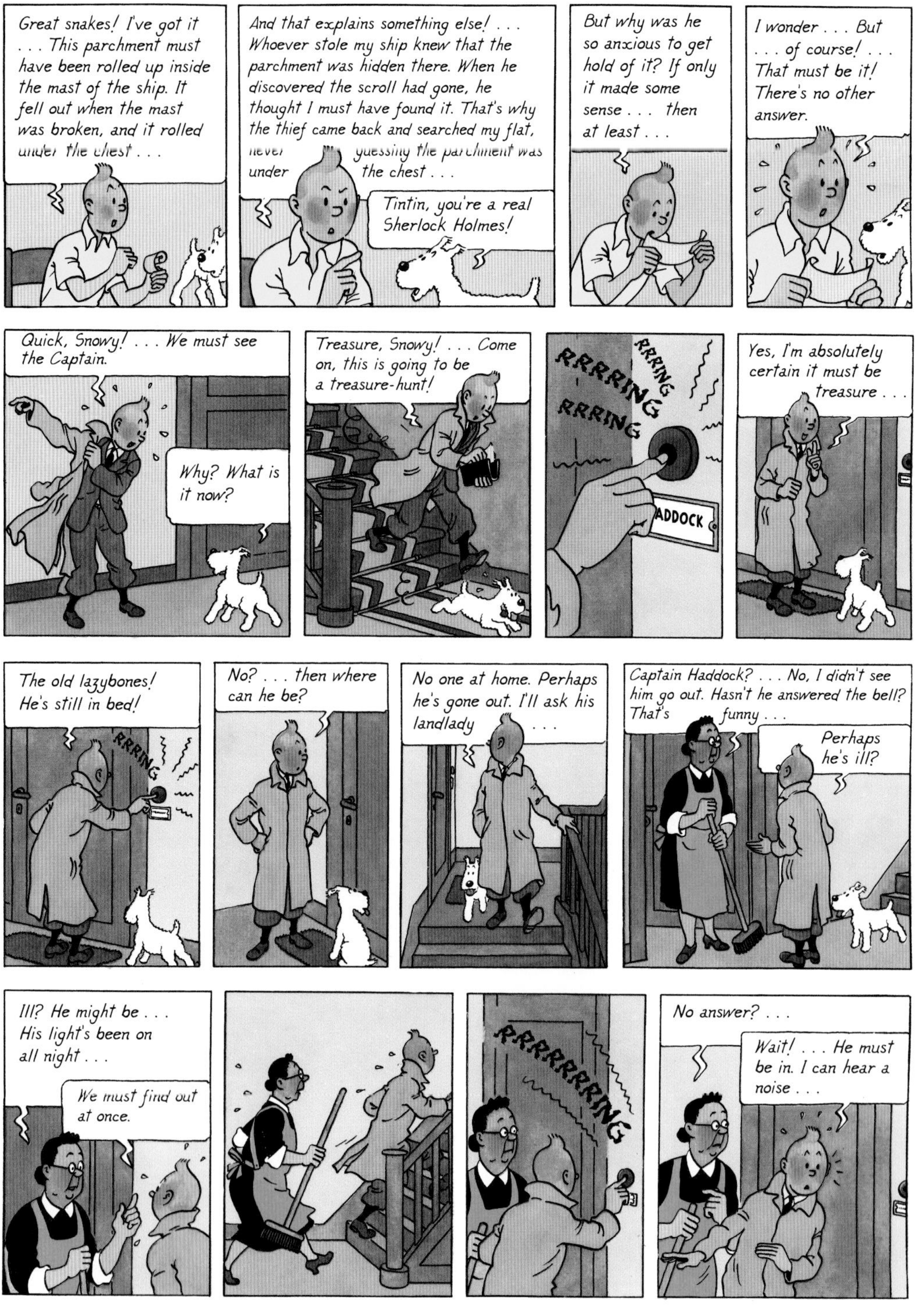
Great snakes! I've got it . . . This parchment must have been rolled up inside the mast of the ship. It fell out when the mast was broken, and it rolled under the chest . . .
And that explains something else! . . . Whoever stole my ship knew that the parchment was hidden there. When he discovered the scroll had gone, he thought I must have found it. That's why the thief came back and searched my flat, never guessing the parchment was under the chest . . .
Tintin, you're a real Sherlock Holmes!
But why was he so anxious to get hold of it? If only it made some sense . . . then at least . . .
I wonder . . . But . . . of course! . . . That must be it! There's no other answer.
Quick, Snowy! . . . We must see the Captain.
Why? What is it now?
Treasure, Snowy! . . . Come on, this is going to be a treasure-hunt!
RRRING
RRRING
RRRING
ADDOCK
Yes, I'm absolutely certain it must be treasure . . .
The old lazybones! He's still in bed!
RRRING
No? . . . then where can he be?
No one at home. Perhaps he's gone out. I'll ask his landlady . . .
Captain Haddock? . . . No, I didn't see him go out. Hasn't he answered the bell? That's funny . . .
Perhaps he's ill?
Ill? He might be . . . His light's been on all night . . .
We must find out at once.
RRRRRRRING
No answer? . . .
Wait! . . . He must be in. I can hear a noise . . .

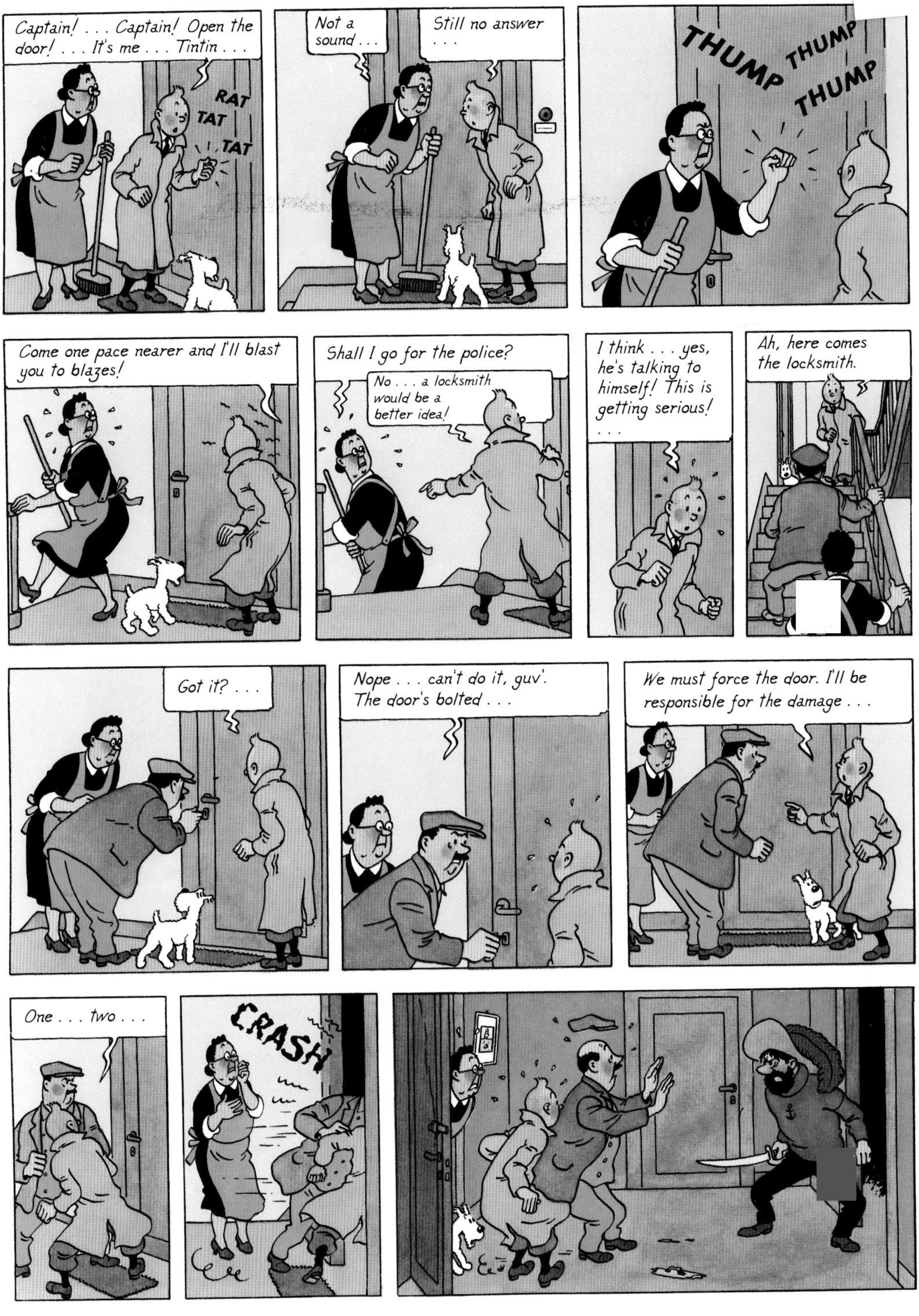
Captain! . . . Captain! Open the door! . . . It's me . . . Tintin . . .
RAT TAT TAT
Not a sound . . .
Still no answer . . .
THUMP THUMP THUMP
Come one pace nearer and I'll blast you to blazes!
Shall I go for the police?
No . . . a locksmith would be a better idea!
I think . . . yes, he's talking to himself! This is getting serious! . . .
Ah, here comes the locksmith.
Got it? . . .
Nope . . . can't do it, guv'. The door's bolted . . .
We must force the door. I'll be responsible for the damage . . .
One . . . two . . .
CRASH

Avast, pirates! Avast there!

Captain! . . .

Avast, you dogs! . . . Sea-gherkins! . . . Baboons!

Buccaneers! . . . Fili-busters! . . . Bagpipers! . . . Gallows-fodder!

We've won! . . . That's got them on the run! . . . With a yo-ho-ho and a bottle of rum!

What's all this play-acting for?

Play-acting? . . . This isn't a play! . . . Come in, and you'll understand . . .

You see that man?

Yes, he's one of your ancestors. What about it?

Well, last night, when I was thinking about this strange business of the ships, I suddenly remembered that up in the attic I had an old sea-chest belonging to my ancestor. This is it . . .

In the chest I found this hat and cutlass, and also . . .

I know! Treasure! . . . Or a treasure-map!

No, not treasure, but something like it! . . . Old manuscripts by Sir Francis Haddock . . . Look, I started reading them yester-day evening, and read all night . . .

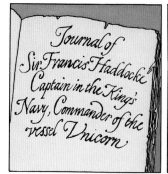
Journal of Sir Francis Haddock Captain in the King's Navy, Commander of the vessel Unicorn

I was still reading when you came in. That's why you found me a little . . . over-excited. But what a story! Just listen to it!

It is the year 1676. The UNICORN, a valiant ship of King Charles II's fleet, has left Barbados in the West Indies, and set sail for home. She carries a cargo of . . . well, anyway, there's a good deal of rum aboard . . .

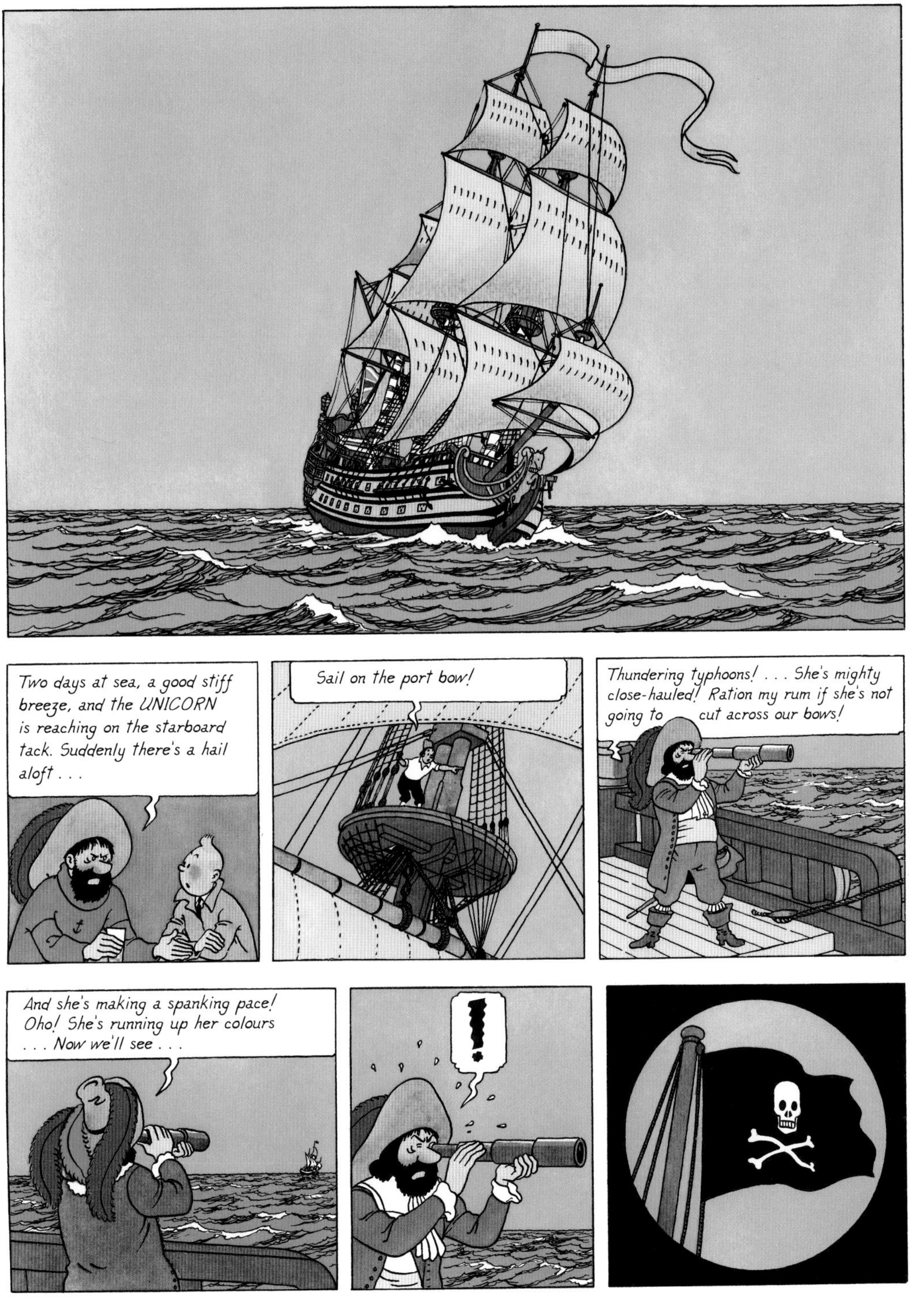
Two days at sea, a good stiff breeze, and the UNICORN is reaching on the starboard tack. Suddenly there's a hail aloft . . .
Sail on the port bow!
Thundering typhoons! . . . She's mighty close-hauled! Ration my rum if she's not going to cut across our bows!
And she's making a spanking pace! Oho! She's running up her colours . . . Now we'll see . . .
!

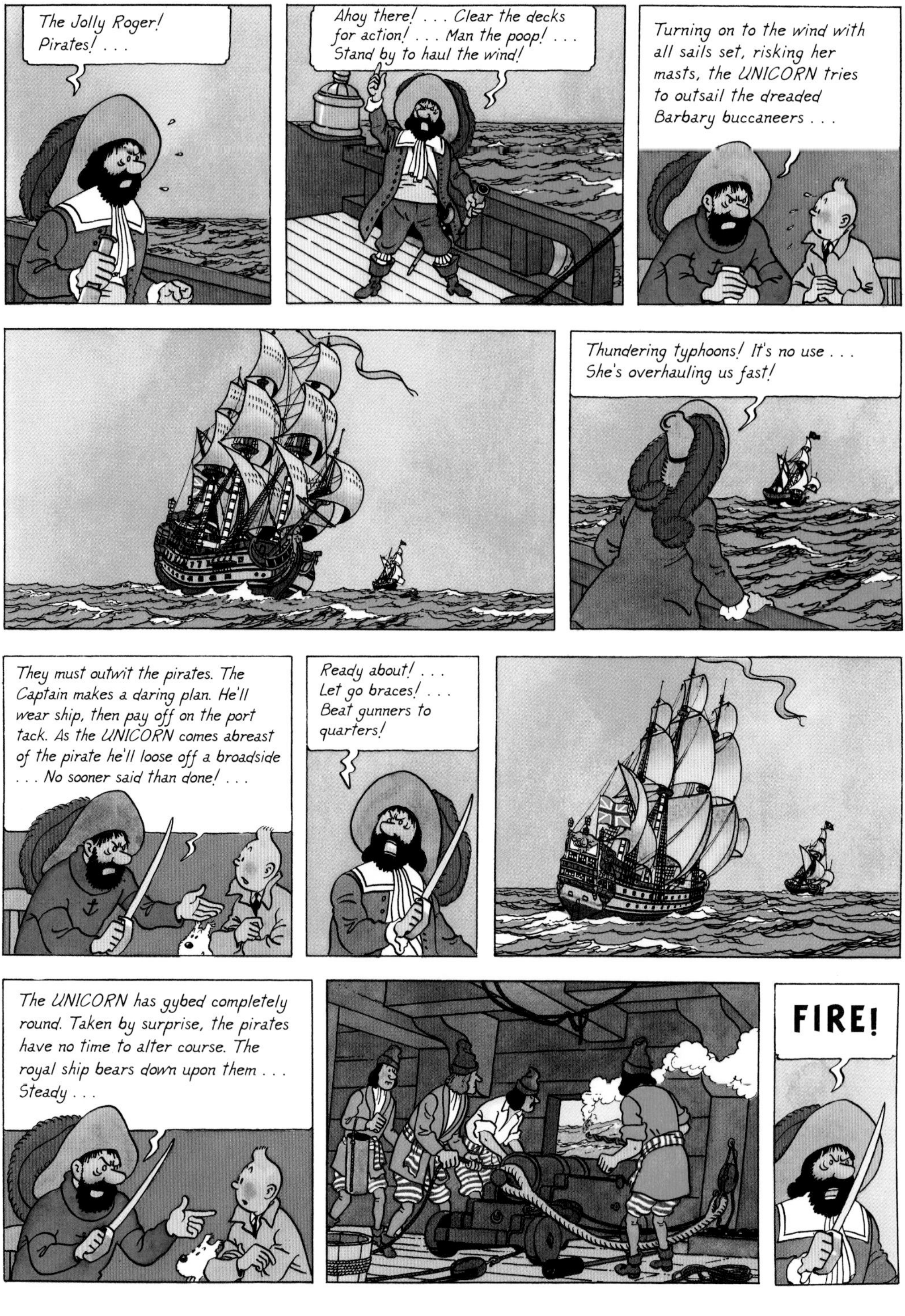
The Jolly Roger! Pirates! . . .
Ahoy there! . . . Clear the decks for action! . . . Man the poop! . . . Stand by to haul the wind!
Turning on to the wind with all sails set, risking her masts, the UNICORN tries to outsail the dreaded Barbary buccaneers . . .
Thundering typhoons! It's no use . . . She's overhauling us fast!
They must outwit the pirates. The Captain makes a daring plan. He'll wear ship, then pay off on the port tack. As the UNICORN comes abreast of the pirate he'll loose off a broadside . . . No sooner said than done! . . .
Ready about! . . . Let go braces! . . . Beat gunners to quarters!
The UNICORN has gybed completely round. Taken by surprise, the pirates have no time to alter course. The royal ship bears down upon them . . . Steady . . .
FIRE!

Got her!

Got her, yes! But not a crippling blow. The pirate ship in turn goes about - and look! She's hoisted fresh colours to the mast-head!

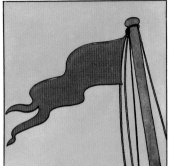

The red pennant! . . . No quarter given! . . . A fight to the death, no prisoners taken! You understand? If we're beaten, then it's every man to Davy Jones's locker!

The pirates take up the chase - they draw closer . . . and closer . . . Throats are dry aboard the UNICORN.

Close hauled, the enemy falls in line astern with the UNICORN, avoiding the fire of her guns . . . She draws closer . . .

Then suddenly, not more than half a cable's length away, she slips from under the UNICORN's poop . . . whoosh, like that!

Then she resumes her course. The two ships are now alongside. The boarders prepare for action . . .

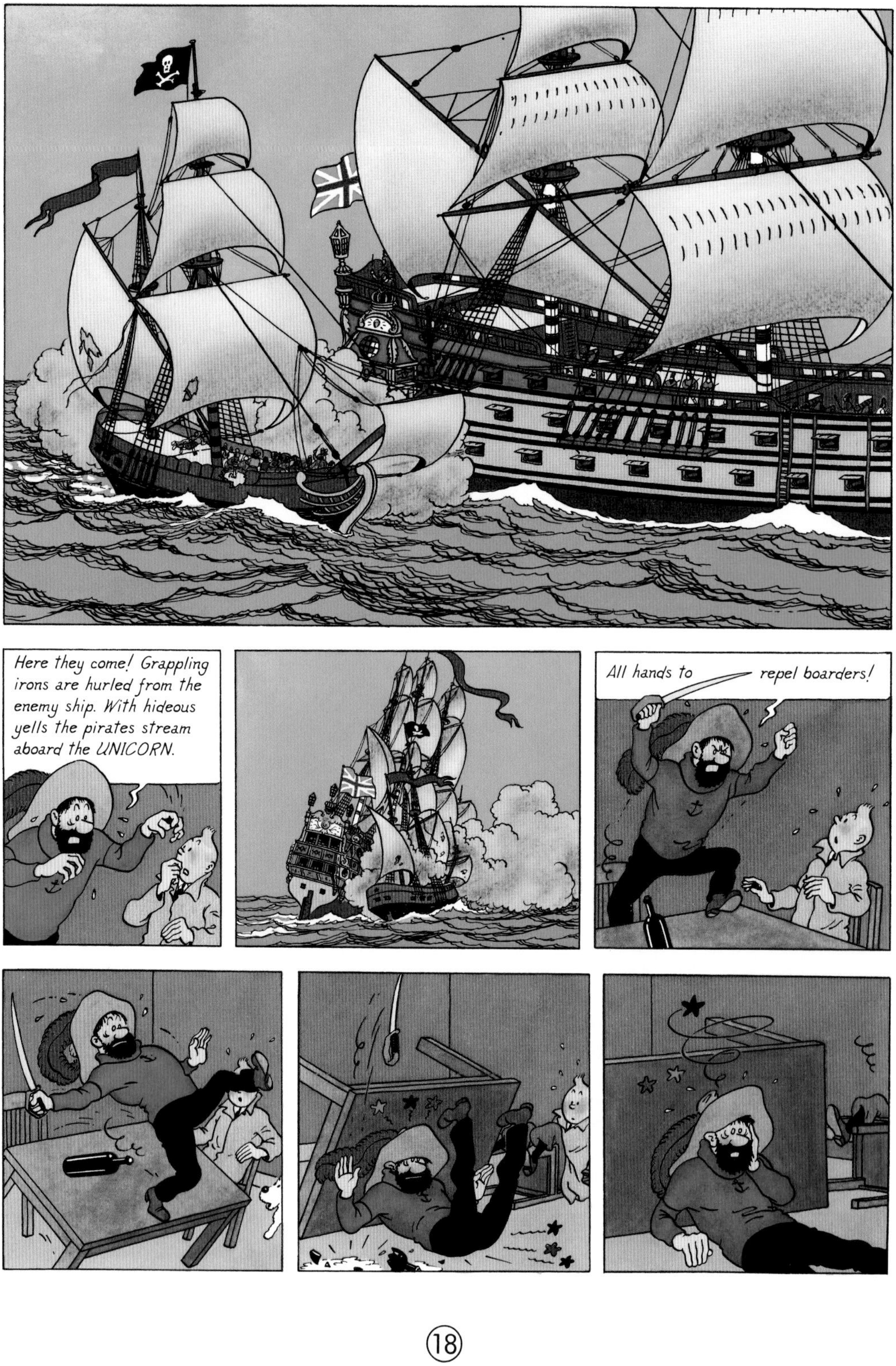
Here they come! Grappling irons are hurled from the enemy ship. With hideous yells the pirates stream aboard the UNICORN.
All hands to repel boarders!

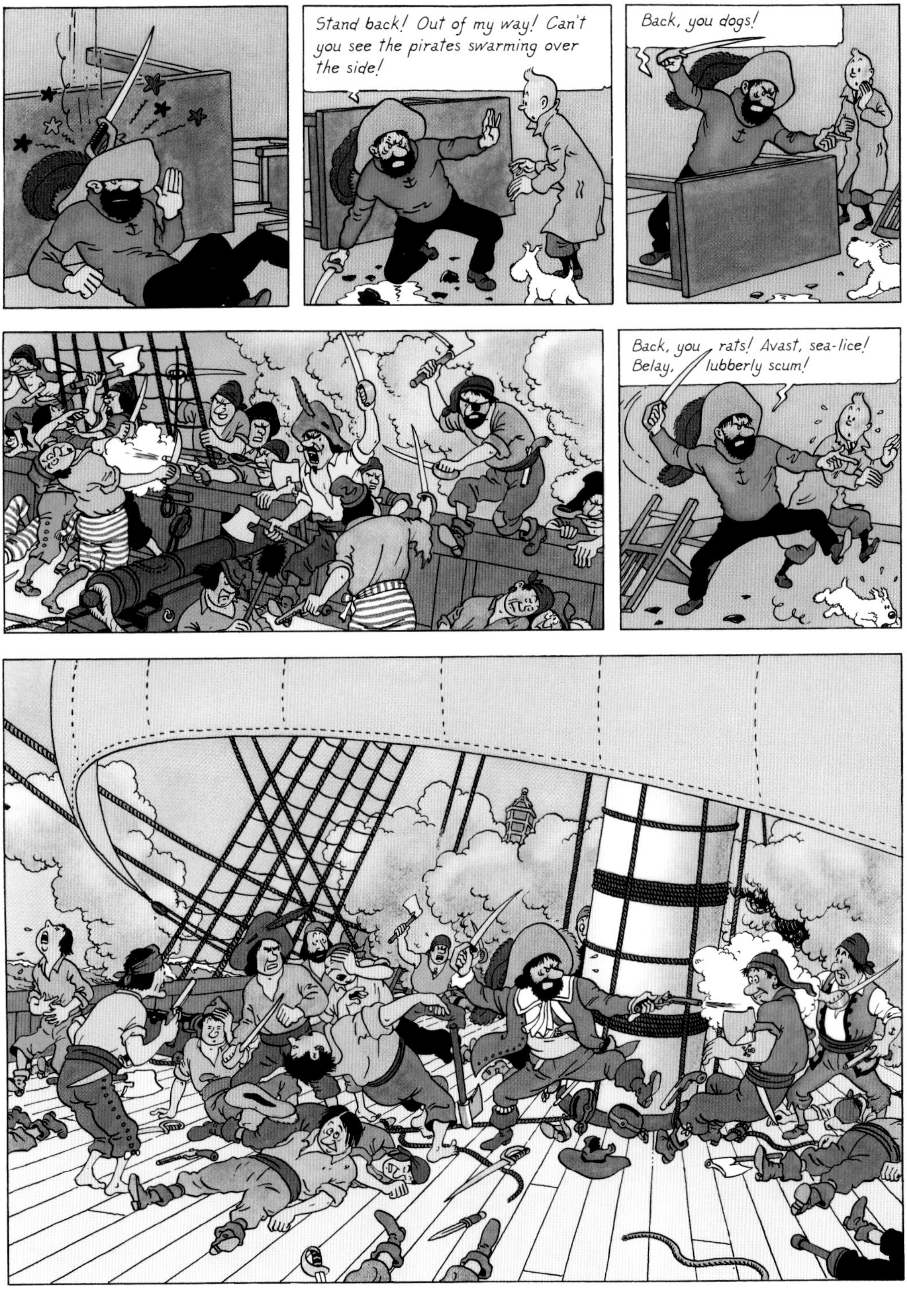
Stand back! Out of my way! Can't you see the pirates swarming over the side!
Back, you dogs!
Back, you rats! Avast, sea-lice! Belay, lubberly scum!

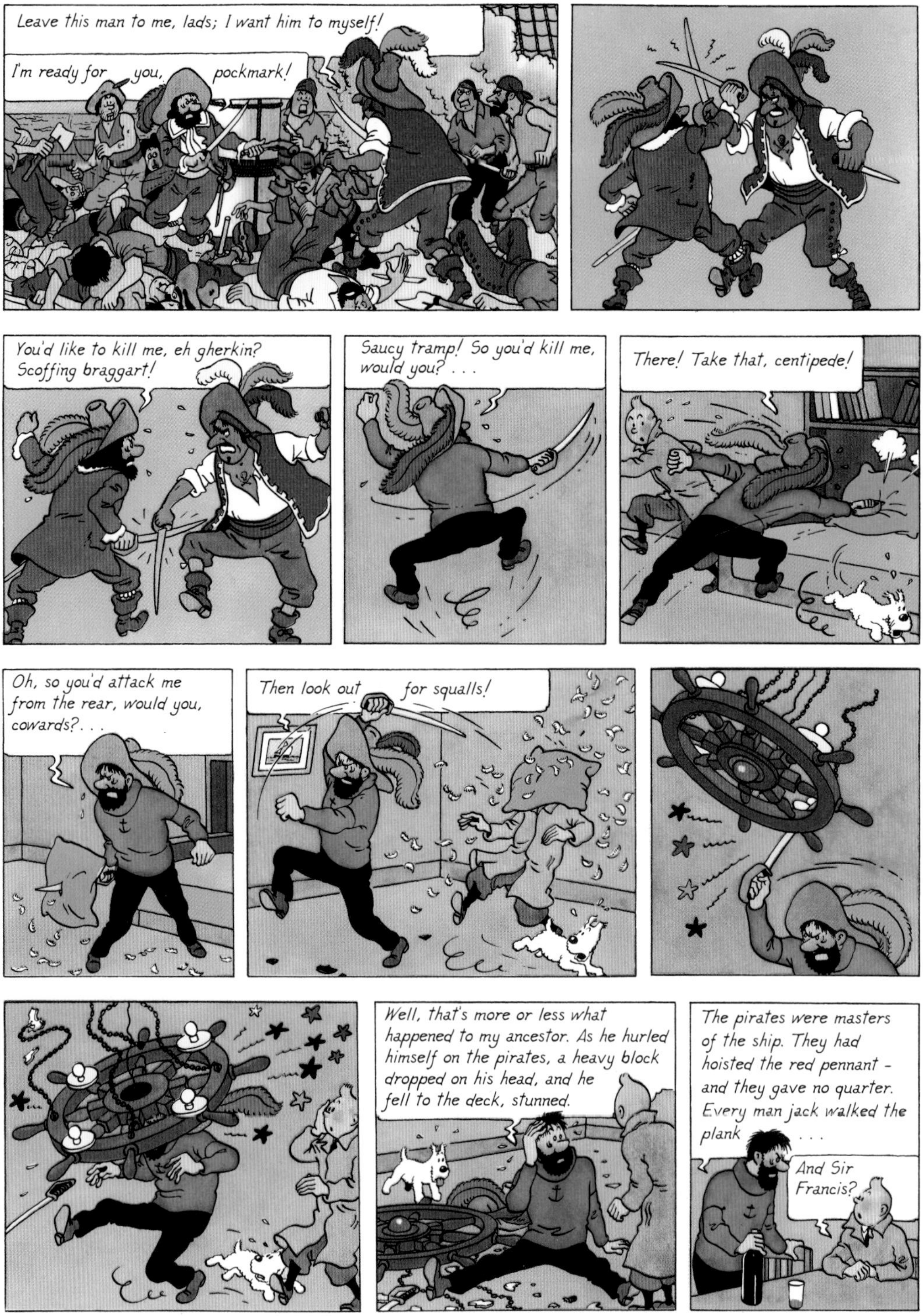

Leave this man to me, lads; I want him to myself!
I'm ready for you, pockmark!
You'd like to kill me, eh gherkin? Scoffing braggart!
Saucy tramp! So you'd kill me, would you? . . .
There! Take that, centipede!
Oh, so you'd attack me from the rear, would you, cowards?. . .
Then look out for squalls!
Well, that's more or less what happened to my ancestor. As he hurled himself on the pirates, a heavy block dropped on his head, and he fell to the deck, stunned.
The pirates were masters of the ship. They had hoisted the red pennant - and they gave no quarter. Every man jack walked the plank . . .
And Sir Francis?

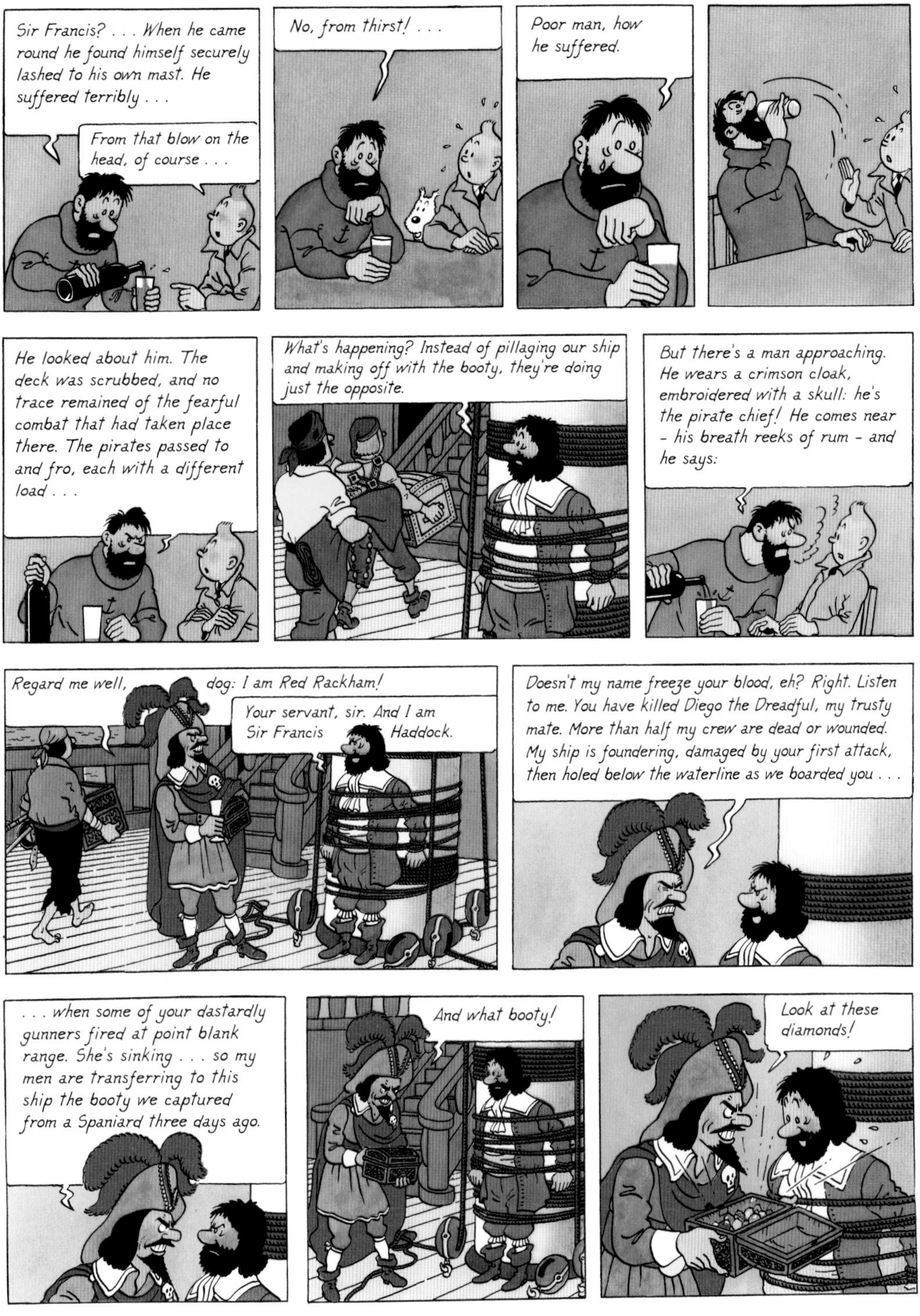
Sir Francis? . . . When he came round he found himself securely lashed to his own mast. He suffered terribly . . .
From that blow on the head, of course . . .
No, from thirst! . . .
Poor man, how he suffered.
He looked about him. The deck was scrubbed, and no trace remained of the fearful combat that had taken place there. The pirates passed to and fro, each with a different load . . .
What's happening? Instead of pillaging our ship and making off with the booty, they're doing just the opposite.
But there's a man approaching. He wears a crimson cloak, embroidered with a skull: he's the pirate chief! He comes near - his breath reeks of rum - and he says:
Regard me well, dog: I am Red Rackham!
Your servant, sir. And I am Sir Francis Haddock.
Doesn't my name freeze your blood, eh? Right. Listen to me. You have killed Diego the Dreadful, my trusty mate. More than half my crew are dead or wounded. My ship is foundering, damaged by your first attack, then holed below the waterline as we boarded you . . .
. . . when some of your dastardly gunners fired at point blank range. She's sinking . . . so my men are transferring to this ship the booty we captured from a Spaniard three days ago.
And what booty!
Look at these diamonds!

These are worth more than six times a king's ransom . . .

Did you come here just to tell me that?

No, that's not why I came. I came to tell you that those who annoy me pay dearly for their folly! Tomorrow morning I shall hand you over to my crew. And that flock of lambs know just how to administer a lingering death!

So saying, he laughed sardonically, picked up his glass and drained it at a gulp, like this . . .

That's enough, Captain! Go on with your story . . .

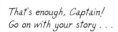

Very well. Towards nightfall, the UNICORN with her pirate crew sighted a small island. Soon she dropped anchor in a sheltered cove . . .

Darkness fell; the pirates found the UNICORN's cargo of rum, broached the casks, and made themselves abominably drunk . . .

Abominably! . . . Yes abominably . . . that's the word . . .

Hey, what's the idea? . . . I only wanted to show you . . .

You don't have to, I quite understand.

Just as you like, Tintin . . . Now where was I?

The pirates were abominably drunk . . .

AAAAA-AAAAH!

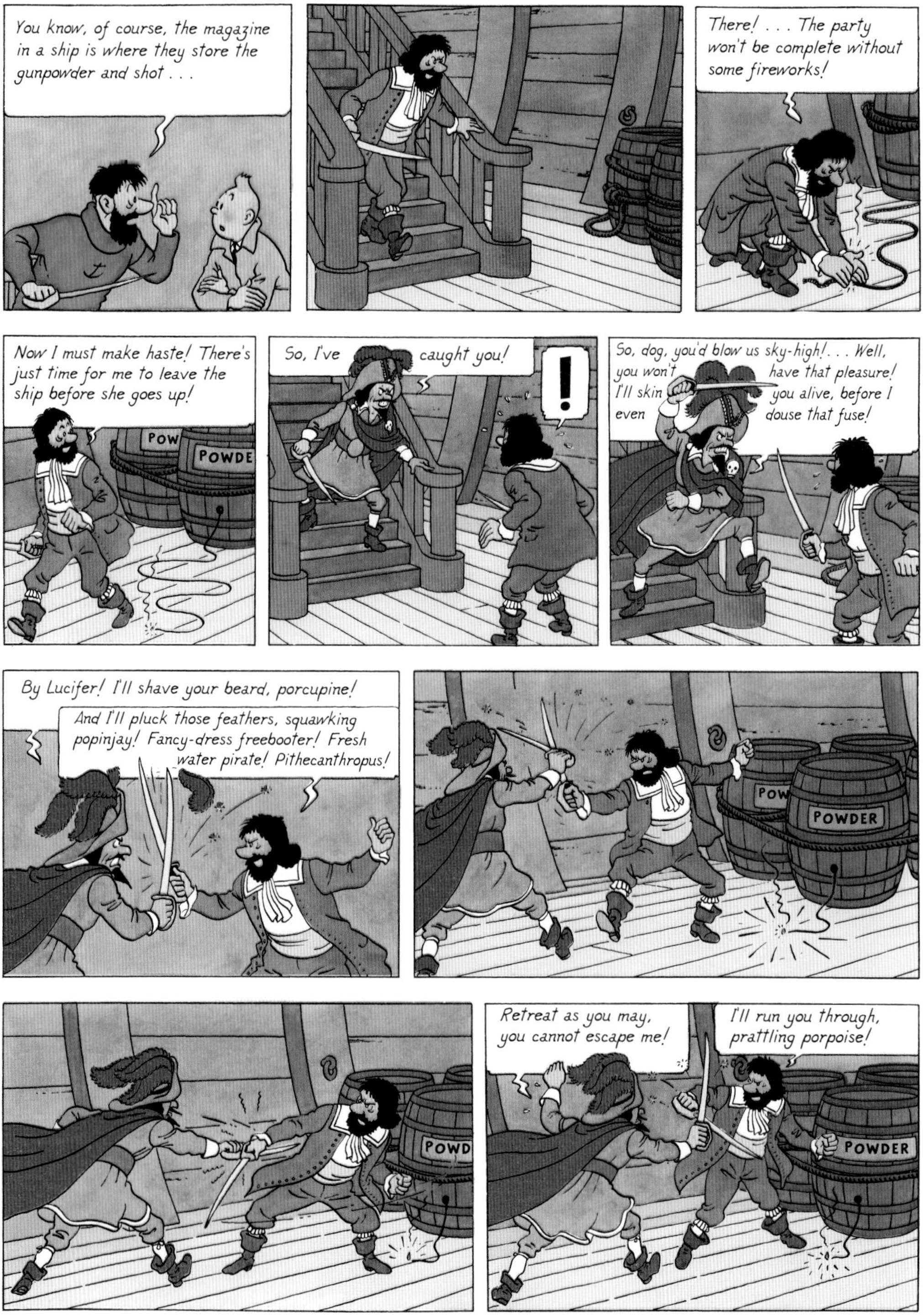
You know, of course, the magazine in a ship is where they store the gunpowder and shot . . .
There! . . . The party won't be complete without some fireworks!
Now I must make haste! There's just time for me to leave the ship before she goes up!
POW
POWDE
So, I've caught you!
!
So, dog, you'd blow us sky-high! . . . Well, you won't have that pleasure! I'll skin you alive, before I even douse that fuse!
By Lucifer! I'll shave your beard, porcupine!
And I'll pluck those feathers, squawking popinjay! Fancy-dress freebooter! Fresh water pirate! Pithecanthropus!
POW
POWDER
POWD
Retreat as you may, you cannot escape me!
I'll run you through, prattling porpoise!
POWDER

And as he fought, Sir Francis kept thinking of that fuse, about to touch off the powder at any moment...

Suddenly, nimbly parrying a thrust, he leapt to one side...

With one swift blow from his heel he extinguished the fuse!

WOOOAH!

Now, Red Rackham, my temper's rising!

BANG
THUMP
ZZINNG
CRACK

Victory! Red Rackham lies dead! With a yo-ho-ho and a bottle of rum!

That's that! May heaven forgive your wicked soul!

Enough delay! Now to light another fuse...

POW
POWDER

... and be off!

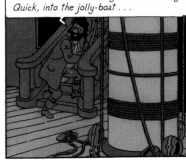

No one has seen me: they're still drinking. Quick, into the jolly-boat...

Jusht look at the j-jolly-boat . . . Ish . . . ish going away . . .

Nonshensh! You're sheeing shings . . . you'sh drunk . . .

Hurrah! Justice is done!

So perished the UNICORN, that stout ship commanded by Sir Francis Haddock. And of all the pirates aboard her, not one escaped with his life . . .

What happened to Sir Francis after that?

He made friends with the natives on the island, and lived among them for two years. Then he was picked up by a ship which carried him back home. There his journal ends. But now comes the strangest thing in the whole story . . .

On the last page of the manuscript there is a sort of Will, in which he bequeaths to each of his three sons a model - built and rigged by himself - a model of the very ship he once blew up rather than leave her to the pirates. There's one funny detail: he tells his sons to move the mainmast slightly aft on each model. "Thus," he concludes, "the truth will out."

That's it, Captain! . . . Red Rackham's treasure will be ours!

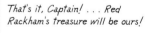

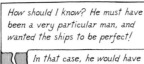

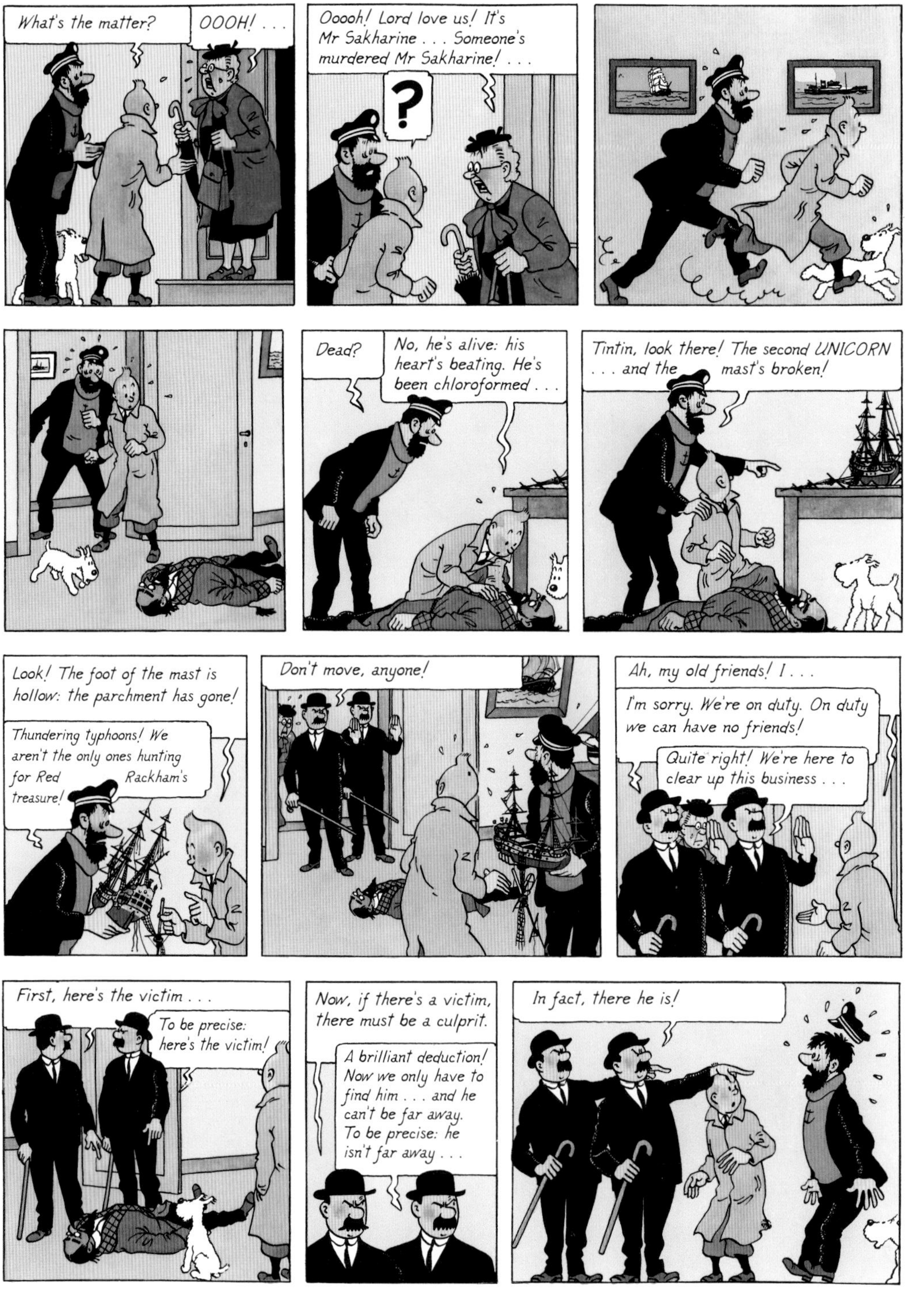
What's the matter?
OOOH! . . .
Ooooh! Lord love us! It's Mr Sakharine . . . Someone's murdered Mr Sakharine! . . .
?
Dead?
No, he's alive: his heart's beating. He's been chloroformed . . .
Tintin, look there! The second UNICORN . . . and the mast's broken!
Look! The foot of the mast is hollow: the parchment has gone!
Thundering typhoons! We aren't the only ones hunting for Red Rackham's treasure!
Don't move, anyone!
Ah, my old friends! I . . .
I'm sorry. We're on duty. On duty we can have no friends!
Quite right! We're here to clear up this business . . .
First, here's the victim . . .
To be precise: here's the victim!
Now, if there's a victim, there must be a culprit.
A brilliant deduction! Now we only have to find him . . . and he can't be far away. To be precise: he isn't far away . . .
In fact, there he is!

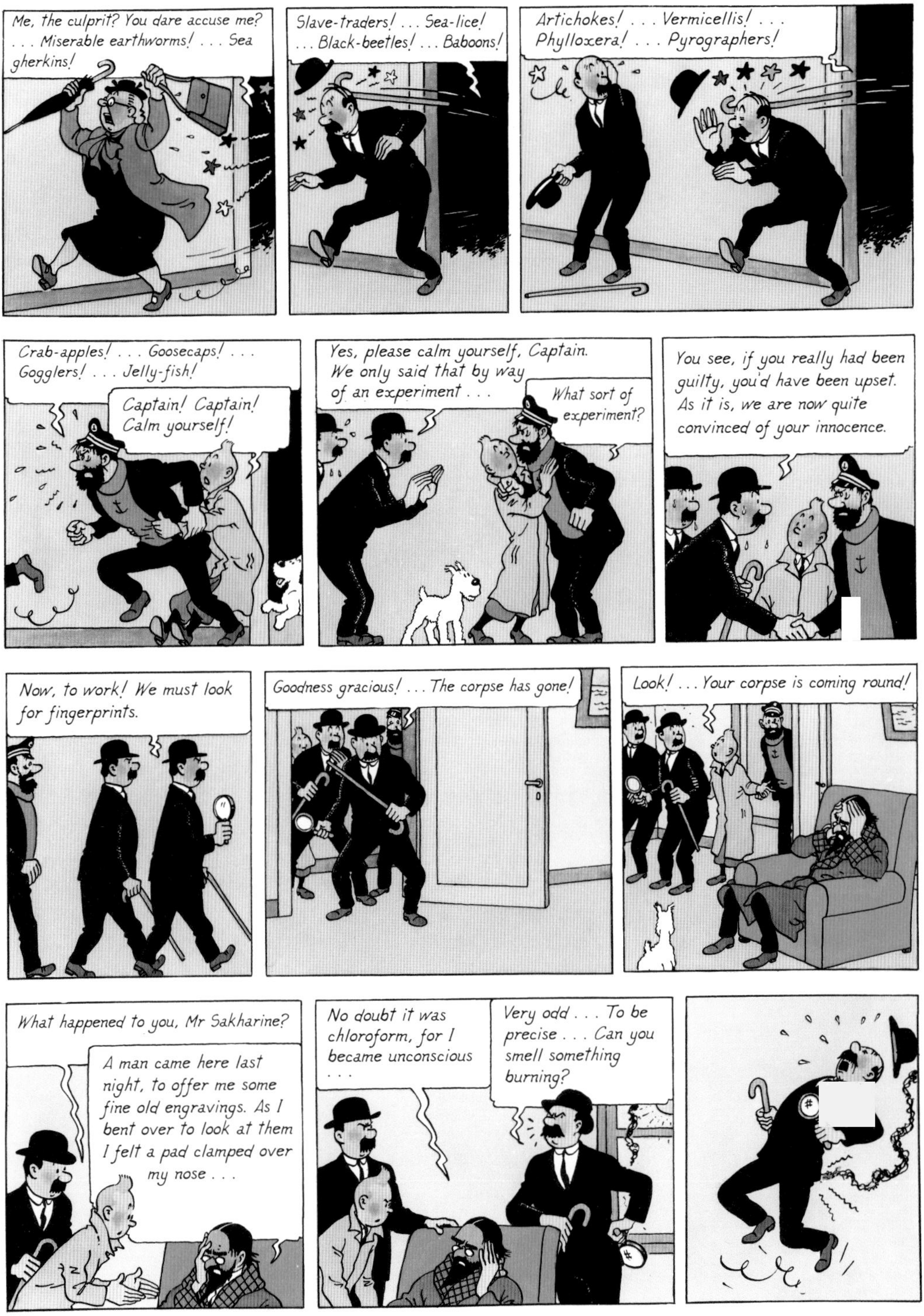
Me, the culprit? You dare accuse me? . . . Miserable earthworms! . . . Sea gherkins!
Slave-traders! . . . Sea-lice! . . . Black-beetles! . . . Baboons!
Artichokes! . . . Vermicellis! . . . Phylloxera! . . . Pyrographers!
Crab-apples! . . . Goosecaps! . . . Gogglers! . . . Jelly-fish!
Captain! Captain! Calm yourself!
Yes, please calm yourself, Captain. We only said that by way of an experiment . . .
What sort of experiment?
You see, if you really had been guilty, you'd have been upset. As it is, we are now quite convinced of your innocence.
Now, to work! We must look for fingerprints.
Goodness gracious! . . . The corpse has gone!
Look! . . . Your corpse is coming round!
What happened to you, Mr Sakharine?
A man came here last night, to offer me some fine old engravings. As I bent over to look at them I felt a pad clamped over my nose . . .
No doubt it was chloroform, for I became unconscious . . .
Very odd . . . To be precise . . . Can you smell something burning?

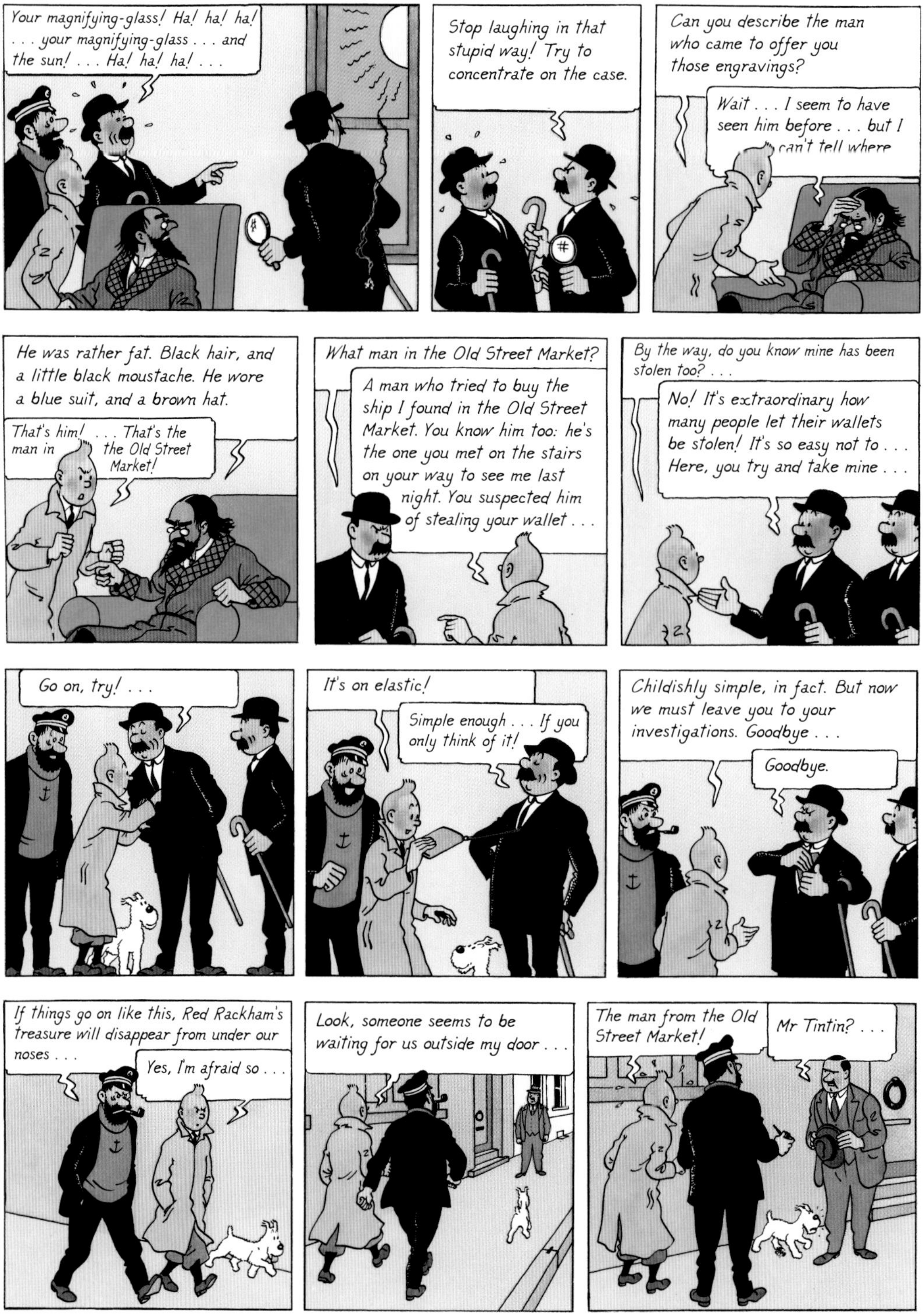
Your magnifying-glass! Ha! ha! ha! . . . your magnifying-glass . . . and the sun! . . . Ha! ha! ha! . . .
Stop laughing in that stupid way! Try to concentrate on the case.
Can you describe the man who came to offer you those engravings?
Wait . . . I seem to have seen him before . . . but I can't tell where
He was rather fat. Black hair, and a little black moustache. He wore a blue suit, and a brown hat.
That's him! . . . That's the man in the Old Street Market!
What man in the Old Street Market?
A man who tried to buy the ship I found in the Old Street Market. You know him too: he's the one you met on the stairs on your way to see me last night. You suspected him of stealing your wallet . . .
By the way, do you know mine has been stolen too? . . .
No! It's extraordinary how many people let their wallets be stolen! It's so easy not to . . . Here, you try and take mine . . .
Go on, try! . . .
It's on elastic!
Simple enough . . . If you only think of it!
Childishly simple, in fact. But now we must leave you to your investigations. Goodbye . . .
Goodbye.
If things go on like this, Red Rackham's treasure will disappear from under our noses . . .
Yes, I'm afraid so . . .
Look, someone seems to be waiting for us outside my door . . .
The man from the Old Street Market!
Mr Tintin? . . .

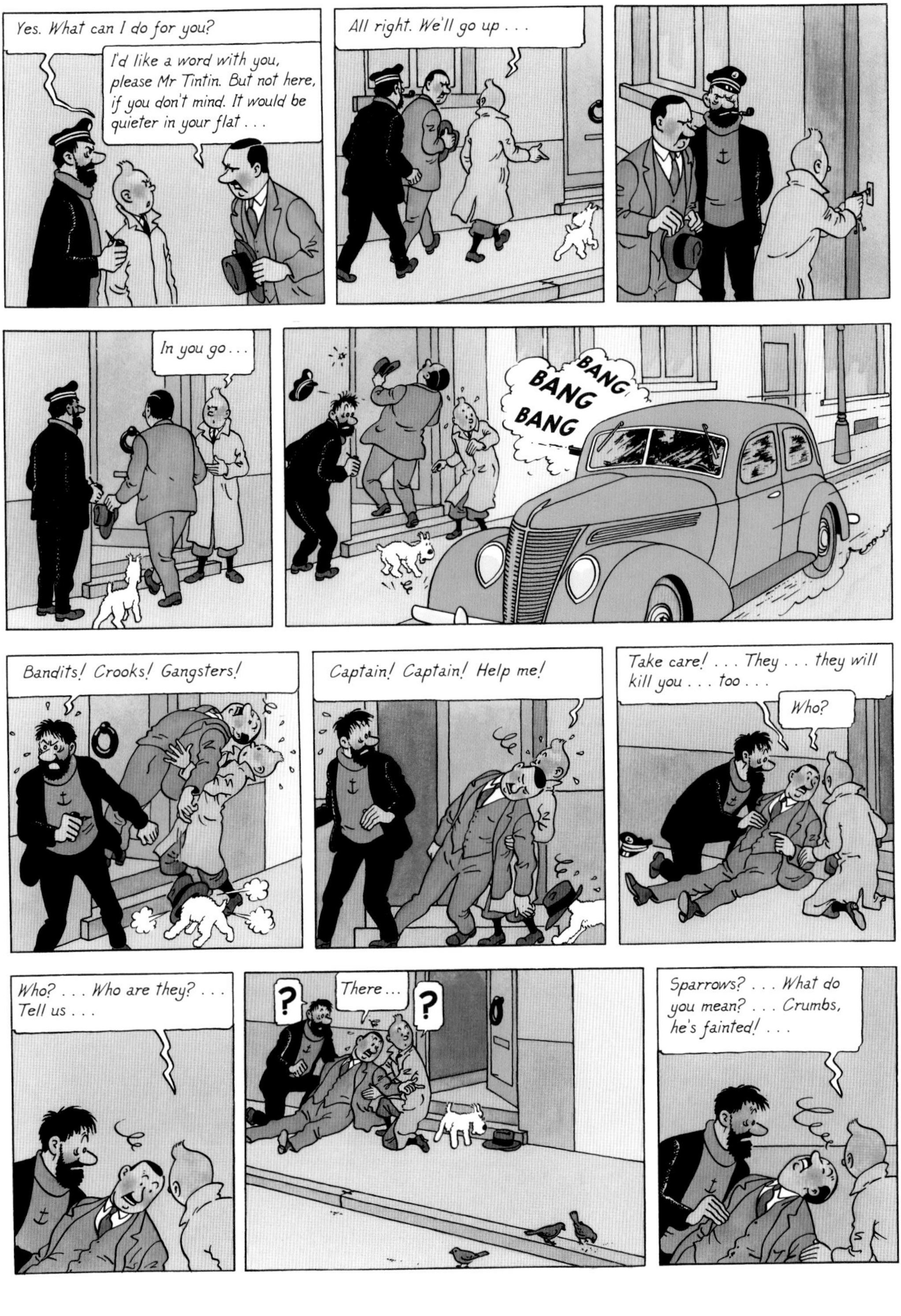
Yes. What can I do for you?
I'd like a word with you, please Mr Tintin. But not here, if you don't mind. It would be quieter in your flat . . .
All right. We'll go up . . .
In you go . . .
BANG
BANG
BANG
BANG
Bandits! Crooks! Gangsters!
Captain! Captain! Help me!
Take care! . . . They . . . they will kill you . . . too . . .
Who?
Who? . . . Who are they? . . . Tell us . . .
?
There . . .
?
Sparrows? . . . What do you mean? . . . Crumbs, he's fainted! . . .

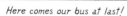

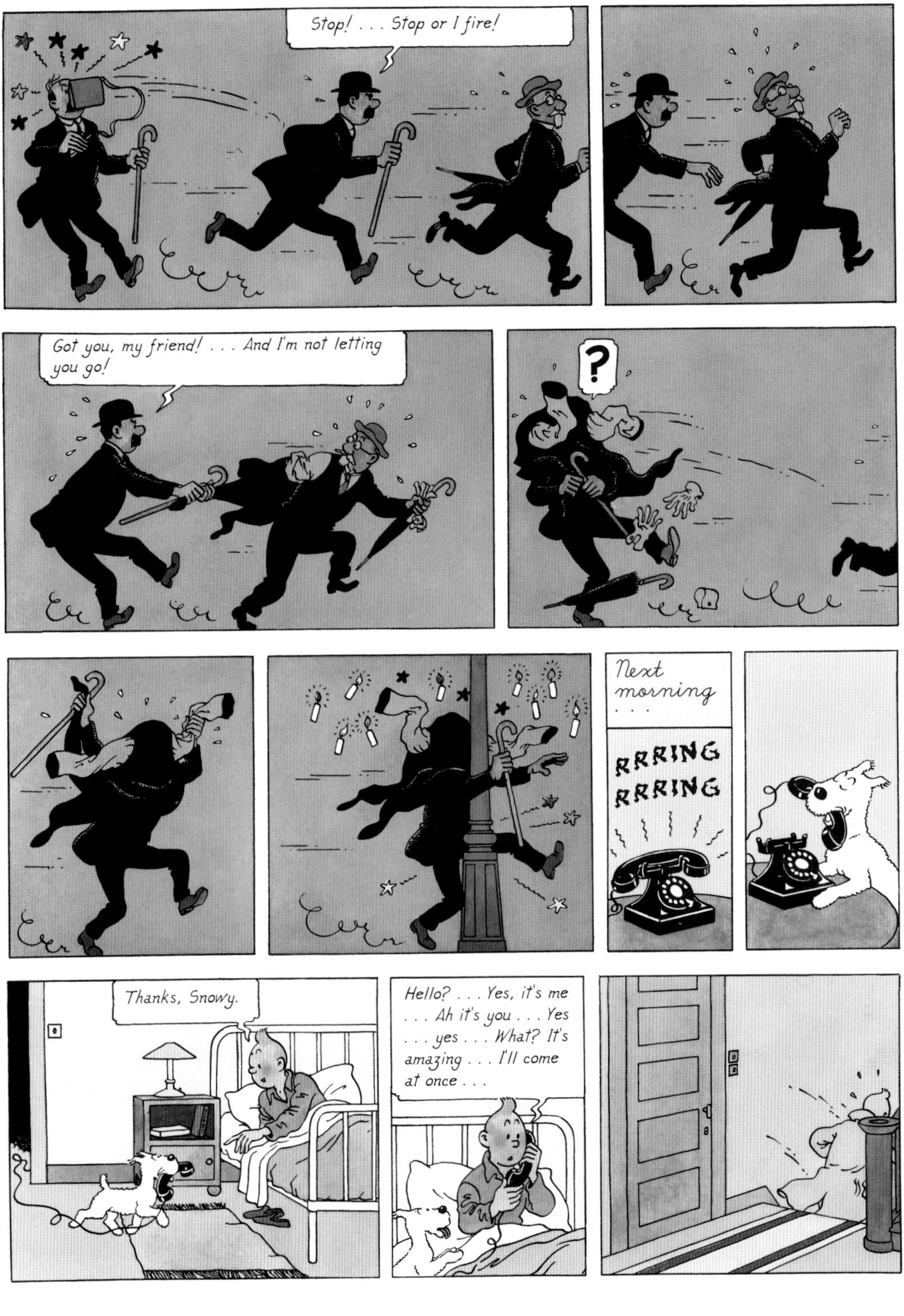
Stop! . . . Stop or I fire!
Got you, my friend! . . . And I'm not letting you go!
?
Next morning . . .
RRRING RRRING
Thanks, Snowy.
Hello? . . . Yes, it's me . . . Ah it's you . . . Yes . . . yes . . . What? It's amazing . . . I'll come at once . . .

Ah, Captain! . . . Come with me . . .

Where? . . .

To see the Thomsons: they've found my wallet!

There's no mistake: it's mine all right.

He had seven in his pockets. The day's takings, no doubt.

?

Here's the parchment from the UNICORN's mast. Look, Captain . . .

Er . . . that's good . . .

Tell me: how did you manage to catch the thief?

Catch him? . . . Well, to be quite honest, we only managed to catch his morning-coat.

Yes, it's certainly a morning-coat. How odd for a pickpocket to wear a thing like this.

Isn't it?

The trouble is that the coat doesn't give us any clue about its owner's identity . . .

Doesn't it?

Look at these stitches; they make up a number. That means the coat has been to the cleaners recently.

Goodness, you're right!

So . . . to find the thief's name and address, we've only got to trace the cleaners who use this mark. Quick, we'll make a list of cleaners from the telephone directory, and start hunting for the thief at once!

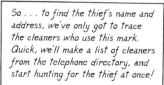

CLEANERS

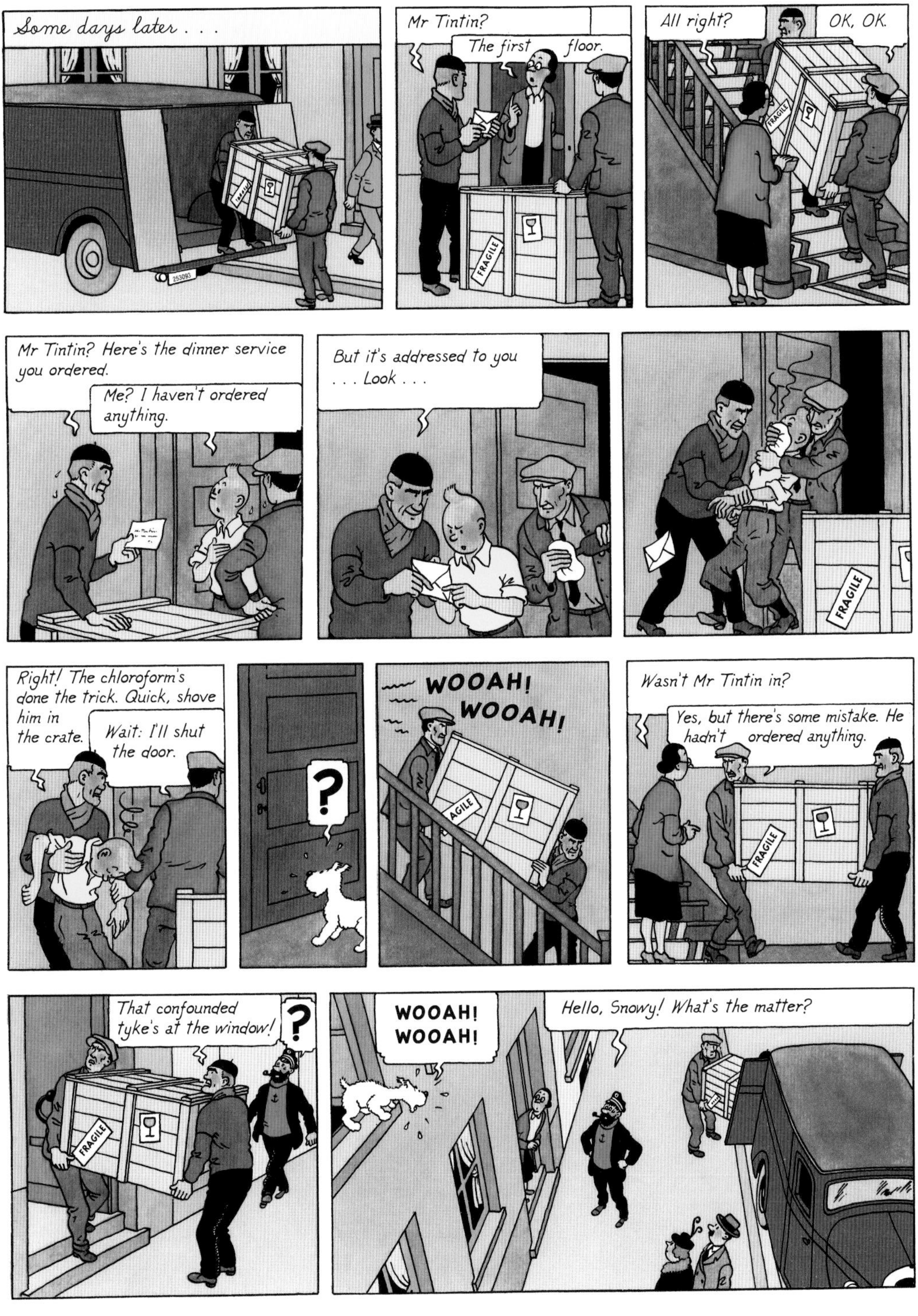
Some days later . . .
Mr Tintin?
The first floor.
All right?
OK, OK.
Mr Tintin? Here's the dinner service you ordered.
Me? I haven't ordered anything.
But it's addressed to you . . . Look . . .
Right! The chloroform's done the trick. Quick, shove him in the crate.
Wait: I'll shut the door.
?
WOOAH! WOOAH!
Wasn't Mr Tintin in?
Yes, but there's some mistake. He hadn't ordered anything.
That confounded tyke's at the window!
?
WOOAH! WOOAH!
Hello, Snowy! What's the matter?

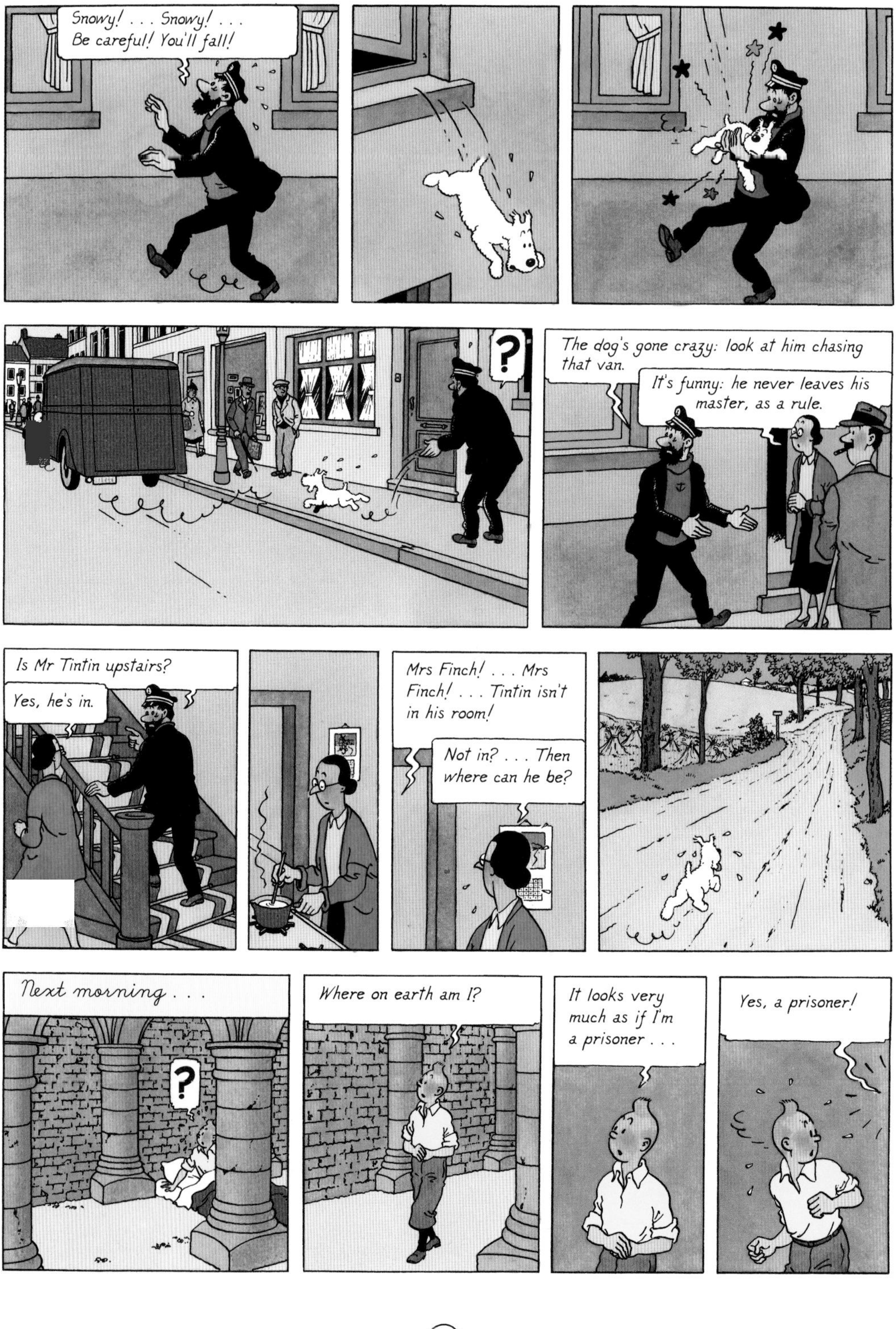
Snowy! . . . Snowy! . . . Be careful! You'll fall!
?
The dog's gone crazy: look at him chasing that van.
It's funny: he never leaves his master, as a rule.
Is Mr Tintin upstairs?
Yes, he's in.
Mrs Finch! . . . Mrs Finch! . . . Tintin isn't in his room!
Not in? . . . Then where can he be?
Next morning . . .
?
Where on earth am I?
It looks very much as if I'm a prisoner . . .
Yes, a prisoner!

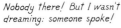

Nobody there! But I wasn't dreaming: someone spoke!

Yes, someone spoke!

Who . . . who are you? . . . And where are you?

Who am I? I am the ghost of the captain of the UNICORN!

Ha! ha! ha! ha! ha!

Ha! ha! ha! . . . That frightened you, didn't it? . . . Come over to the door . . . Come on.

Come nearer. Good . . . Now, can you see the speaking-tube?

Who are you, and what do you want with me?

Who am I? . . . You must allow me to remain anonymous . . . And why did I have you kidnapped? You have guessed that, no doubt . . .

I want to know where you have hidden the two parchments you stole from me.

Me? I stole two parchments? . . . But I never had more than one.

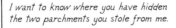

Come on now, let's be sensible! I'd collected two of the three scrolls: you took them from me. That night when I had your flat searched, only the third one was found . . . in your wallet. Where are the other two?

How should I know?

As you like. But I warn you: I know of several ways to loosen stubborn tongues . . . I'll give you two hours to tell me where you hid those scrolls, then if you won't talk, you'll soon see the sort of man I am!

But I tell you . . . Oh he's cut off, the gangster!

Now I'm in a fine mess! How do I get out of this one?

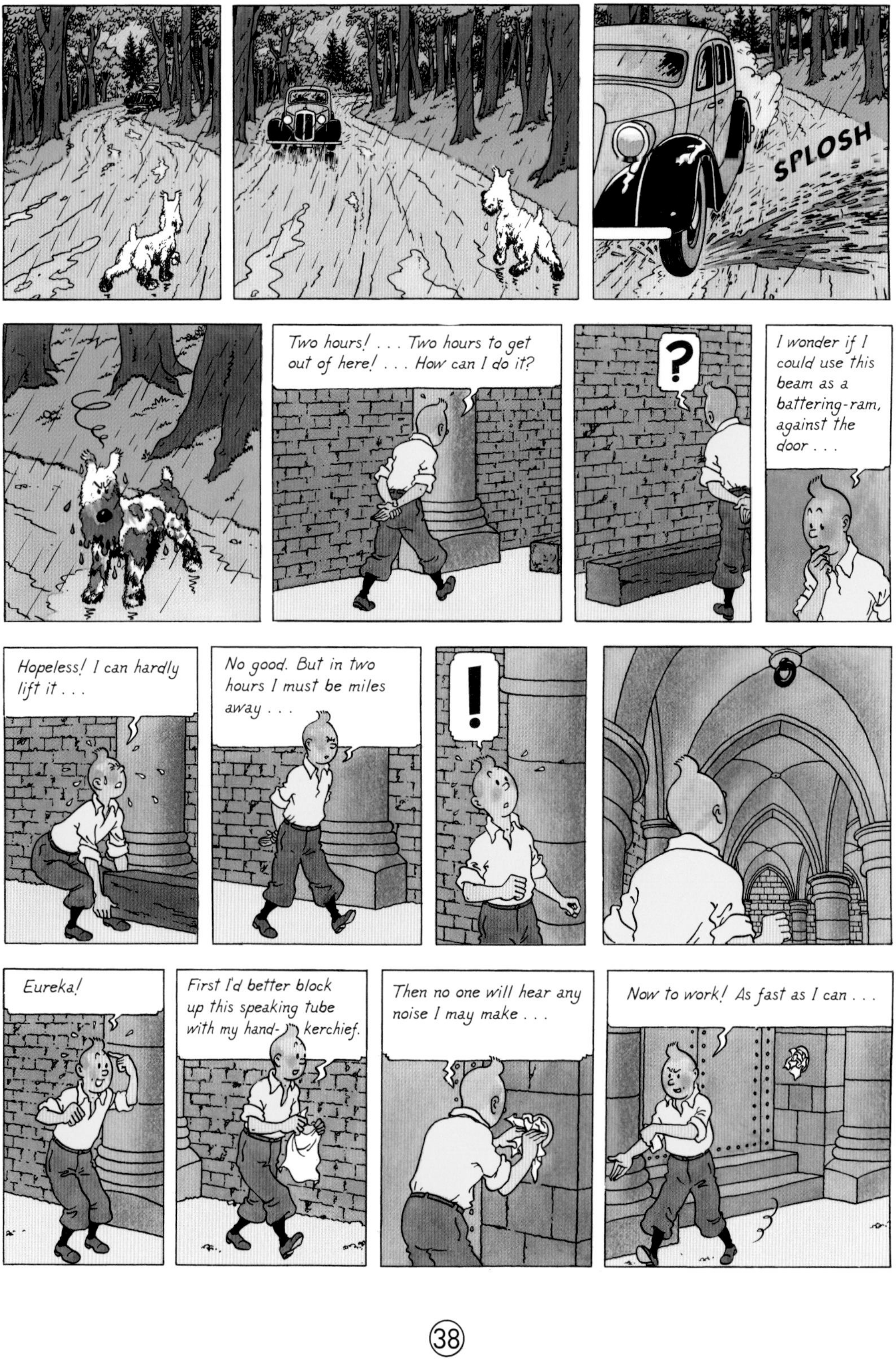
SPLOSH
Two hours! . . . Two hours to get out of here! . . . How can I do it?
?
I wonder if I could use this beam as a battering-ram, against the door . . .
Hopeless! I can hardly lift it . . .
No good. But in two hours I must be miles away . . .
!
Eureka!
First I'd better block up this speaking tube with my hand- kerchief.
Then no one will hear any noise I may make . . .
Now to work! As fast as I can . . .

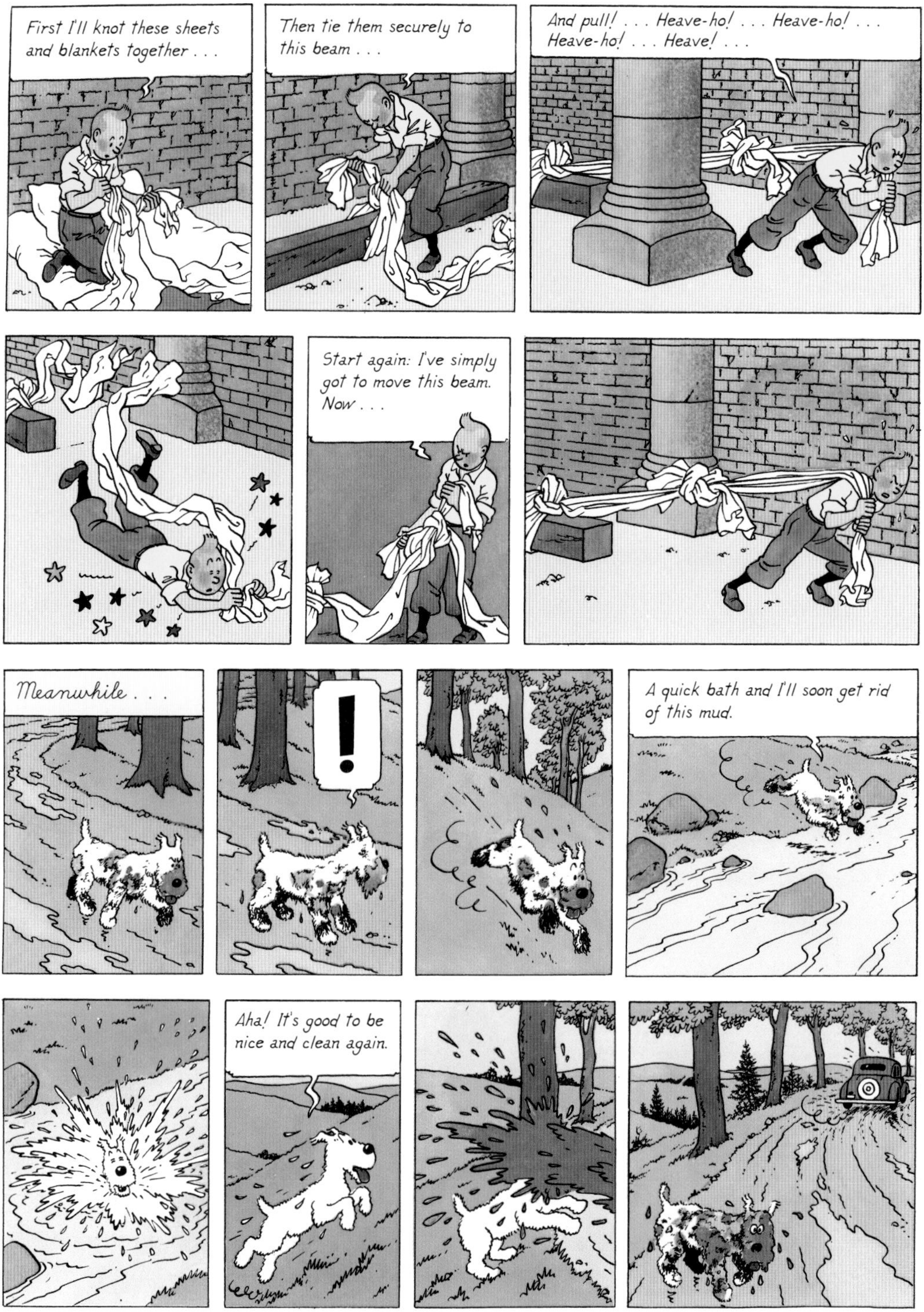
First I'll knot these sheets and blankets together . . .
Then tie them securely to this beam . . .
And pull! . . . Heave-ho! . . . Heave-ho! . . . Heave-ho! . . . Heave! . . .
Start again: I've simply got to move this beam. Now . . .
Meanwhile . . .
!
A quick bath and I'll soon get rid of this mud.
Aha! It's good to be nice and clean again.

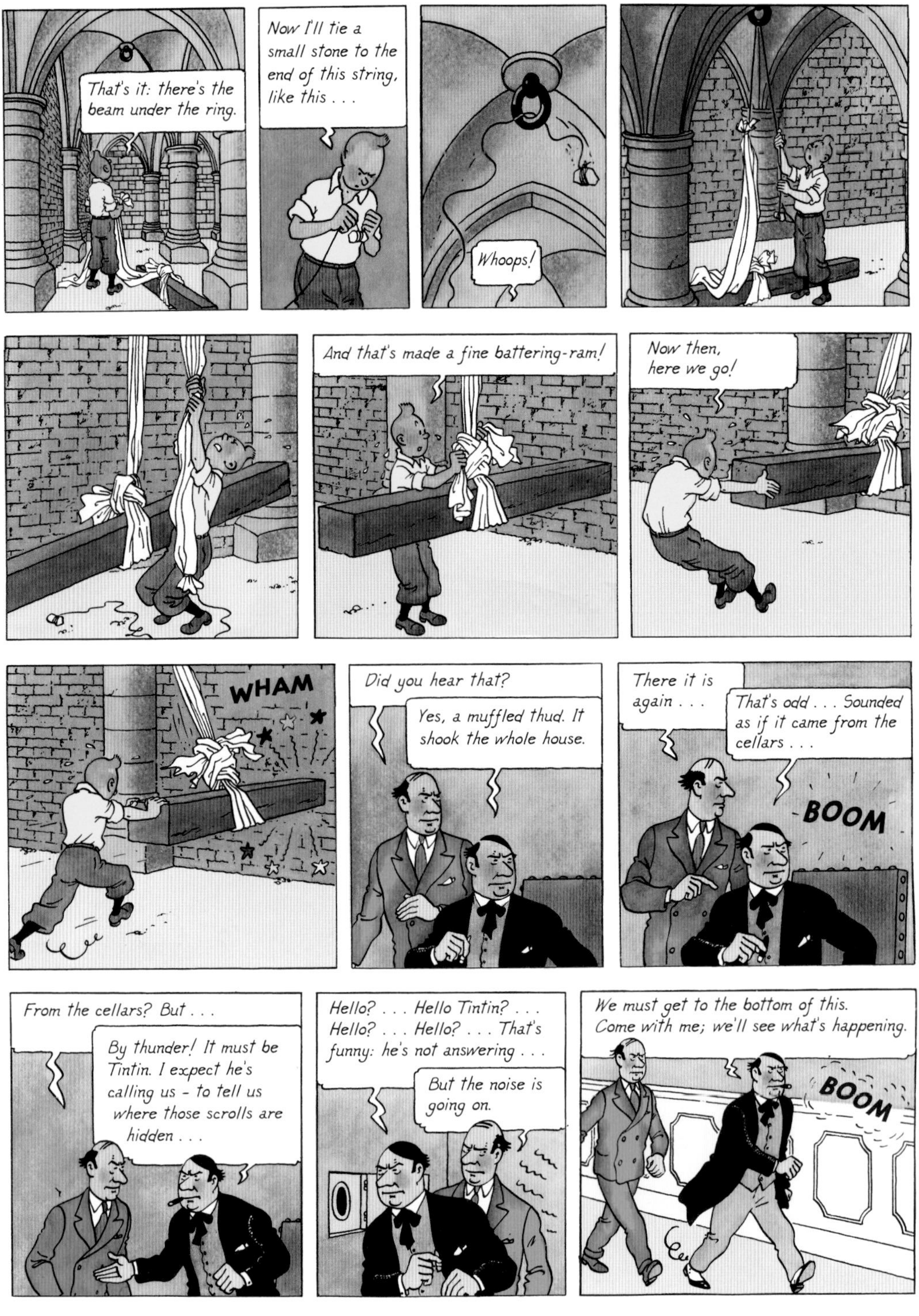
That's it: there's the beam under the ring.
Now I'll tie a small stone to the end of this string, like this . . .
Whoops!
And that's made a fine battering-ram!
Now then, here we go!
WHAM
Did you hear that?
Yes, a muffled thud. It shook the whole house.
There it is again . . .
That's odd . . . Sounded as if it came from the cellars . . .
BOOM
From the cellars? But . . .
By thunder! It must be Tintin. I expect he's calling us - to tell us where those scrolls are hidden . . .
Hello? . . . Hello Tintin? . . . Hello? . . . Hello? . . . That's funny: he's not answering . . .
But the noise is going on.
We must get to the bottom of this. Come with me; we'll see what's happening.
BOOM

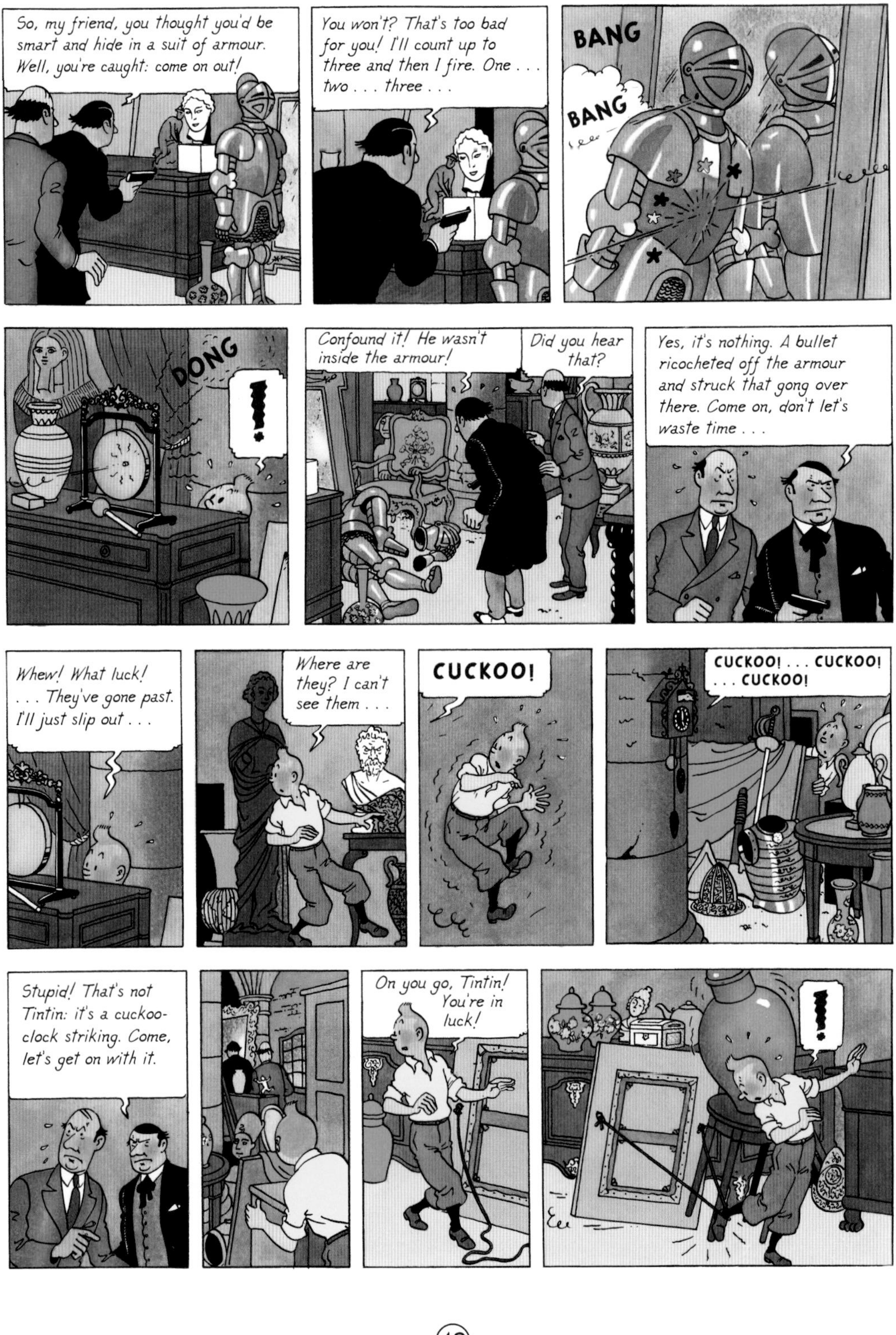
So, my friend, you thought you'd be smart and hide in a suit of armour. Well, you're caught: come on out!
You won't? That's too bad for you! I'll count up to three and then I fire. One . . . two . . . three . . .
BANG
BANG
DONG
!
Confound it! He wasn't inside the armour!
Did you hear that?
Yes, it's nothing. A bullet ricocheted off the armour and struck that gong over there. Come on, don't let's waste time . . .
Whew! What luck! . . . They've gone past. I'll just slip out . . .
Where are they? I can't see them . . .
CUCKOO!
CUCKOO! . . . CUCKOO! . . . CUCKOO!
Stupid! That's not Tintin: it's a cuckoo-clock striking. Come, let's get on with it.
On you go, Tintin! You're in luck!
!

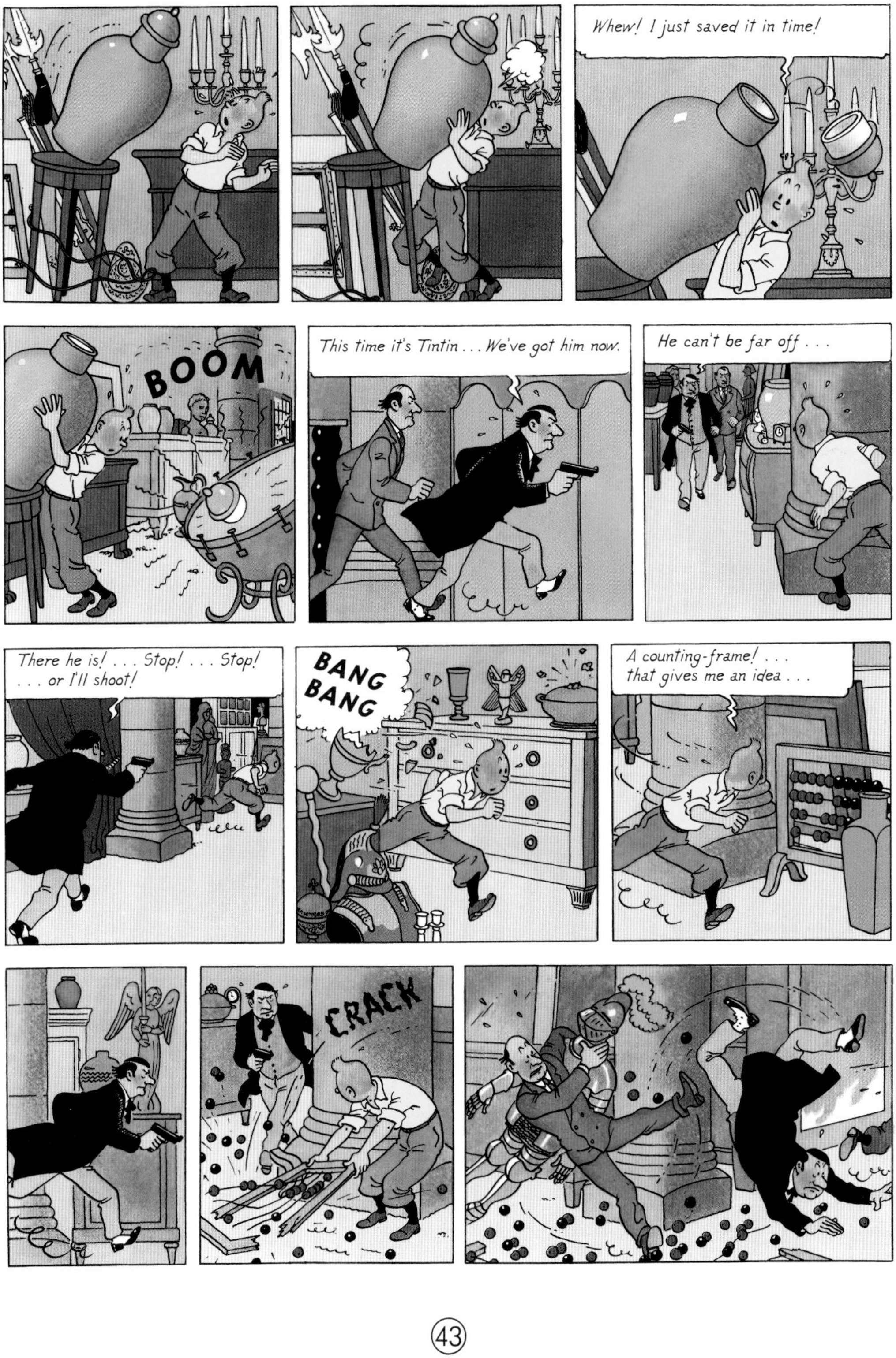
Whew! I just saved it in time!
BOOM
This time it's Tintin . . . We've got him now.
He can't be far off . . .
There he is! . . . Stop! . . . Stop! . . . or I'll shoot!
BANG BANG
A counting-frame! . . . that gives me an idea . . .
CRACK

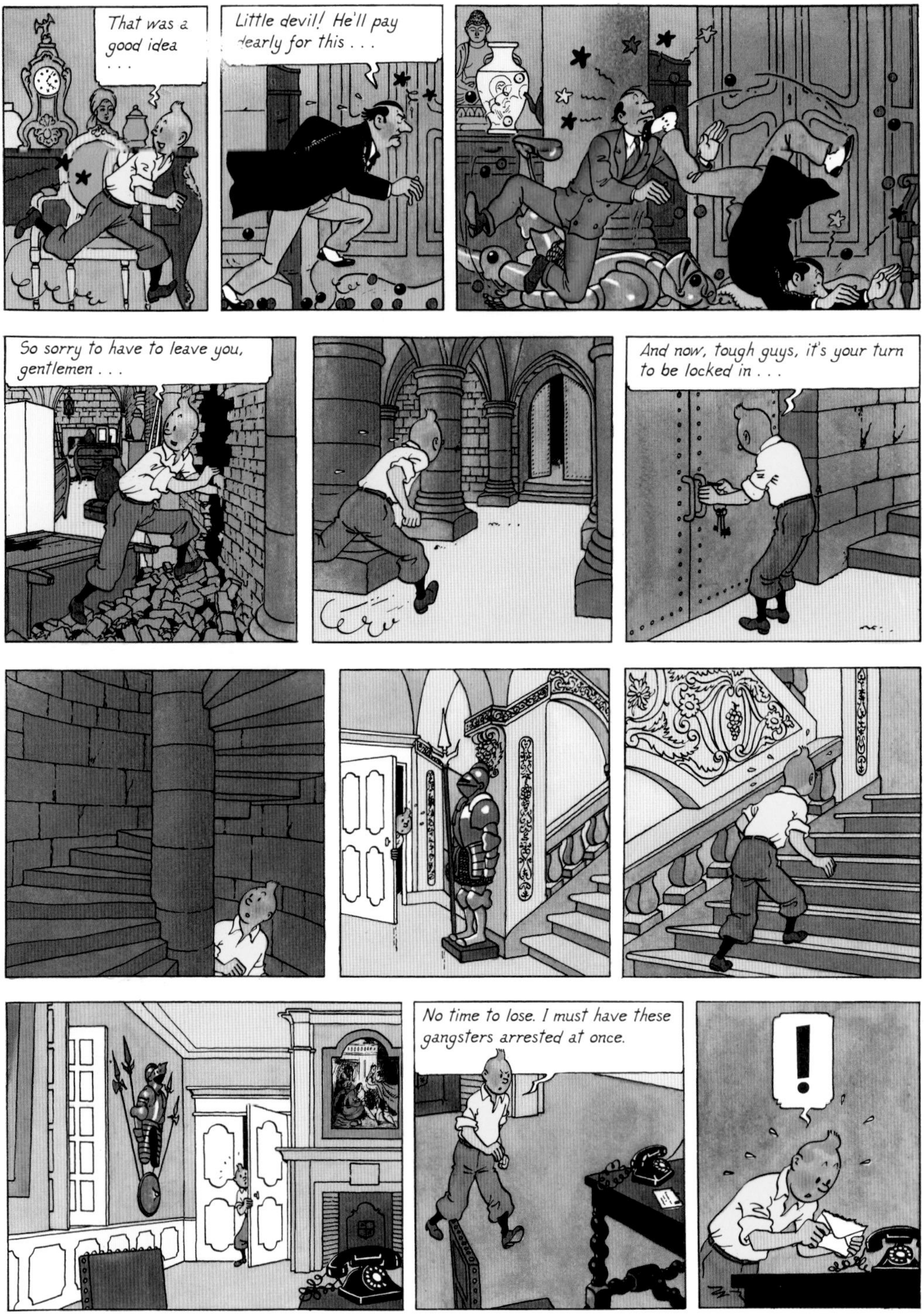

That was a good idea . . .
Little devil! He'll pay dearly for this . . .
So sorry to have to leave you, gentlemen . . .
And now, tough guys, it's your turn to be locked in . . .
No time to lose. I must have these gangsters arrested at once.
!

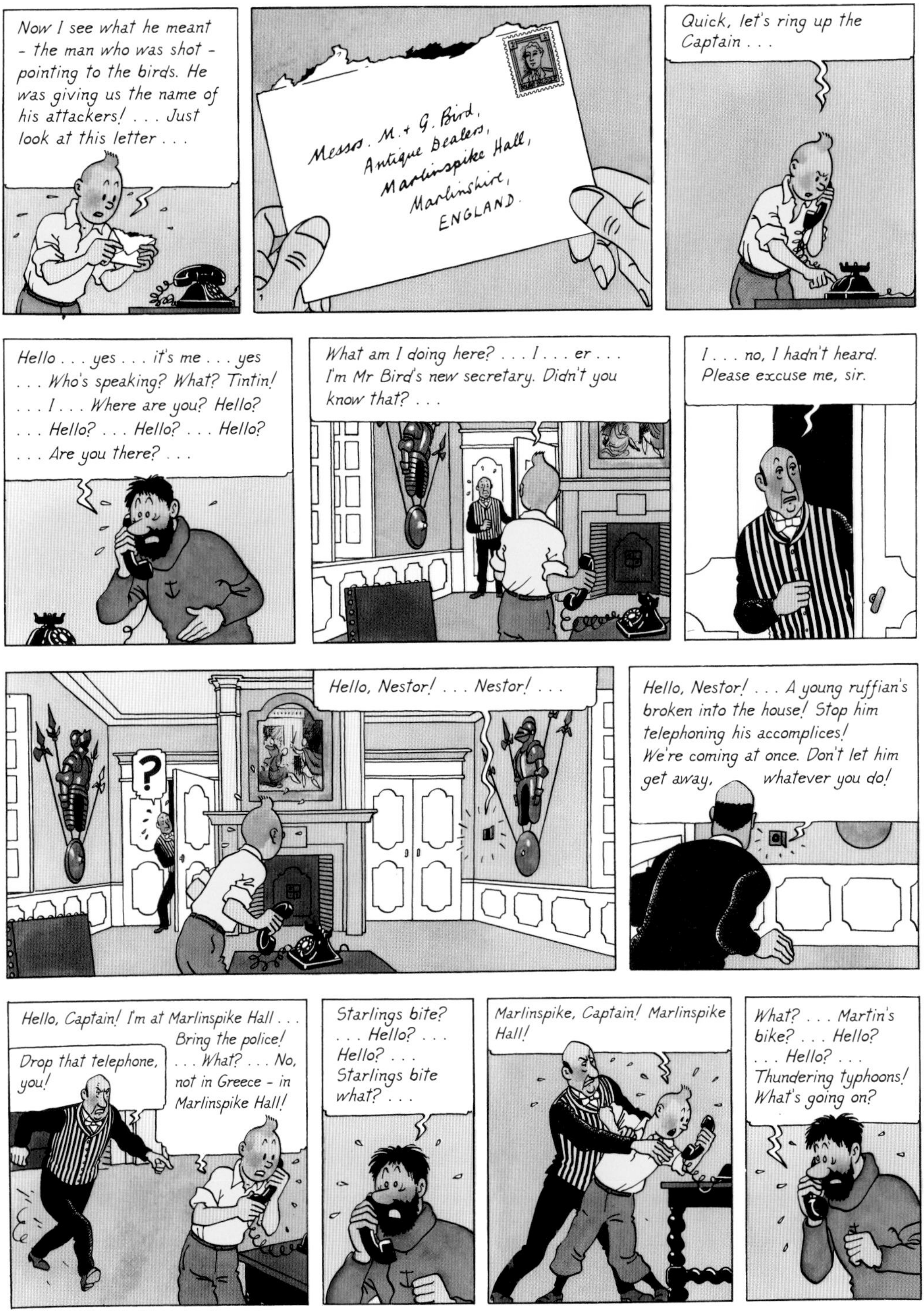
Now I see what he meant - the man who was shot - pointing to the birds. He was giving us the name of his attackers! . . . Just look at this letter . . .
Messrs. M. + G. Bird, Antique Dealers, Marlinspike Hall, Marlinshire, ENGLAND.
Quick, let's ring up the Captain . . .
Hello . . . yes . . . it's me . . . yes . . . Who's speaking? What? Tintin! . . . I . . . Where are you? Hello? . . . Hello? . . . Hello? . . . Hello? . . . Are you there? . . .
What am I doing here? . . . I . . . er . . . I'm Mr Bird's new secretary. Didn't you know that? . . .
I . . . no, I hadn't heard. Please excuse me, sir.
Hello, Nestor! . . . Nestor! . . .
?
Hello, Nestor! . . . A young ruffian's broken into the house! Stop him telephoning his accomplices! We're coming at once. Don't let him get away, whatever you do!
Hello, Captain! I'm at Marlinspike Hall . . . Bring the police! . . . What? . . . No, not in Greece - in Marlinspike Hall!
Drop that telephone, you!
Starlings bite? . . . Hello? . . . Hello? . . . Starlings bite what? . . .
Marlinspike, Captain! Marlinspike Hall!
What? . . . Martin's bike? . . . Hello? . . . Hello? . . . Thundering typhoons! What's going on?

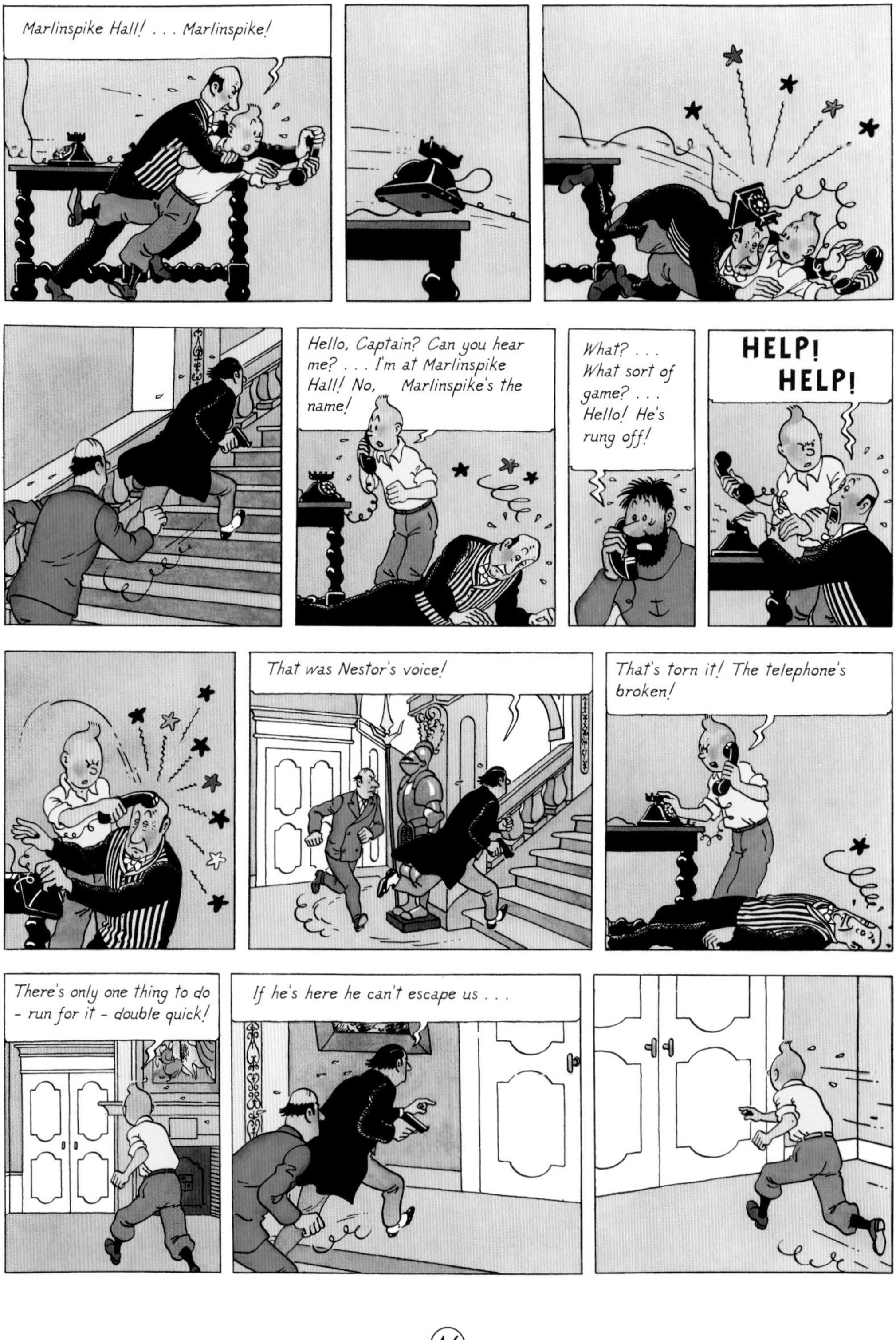

Marlinspike Hall! . . . Marlinspike!
Hello, Captain? Can you hear me? . . . I'm at Marlinspike Hall! No, Marlinspike's the name!
What? . . . What sort of game? . . . Hello! He's rung off!
HELP! HELP!
That was Nestor's voice!
That's torn it! The telephone's broken!
There's only one thing to do - run for it - double quick!
If he's here he can't escape us . . .

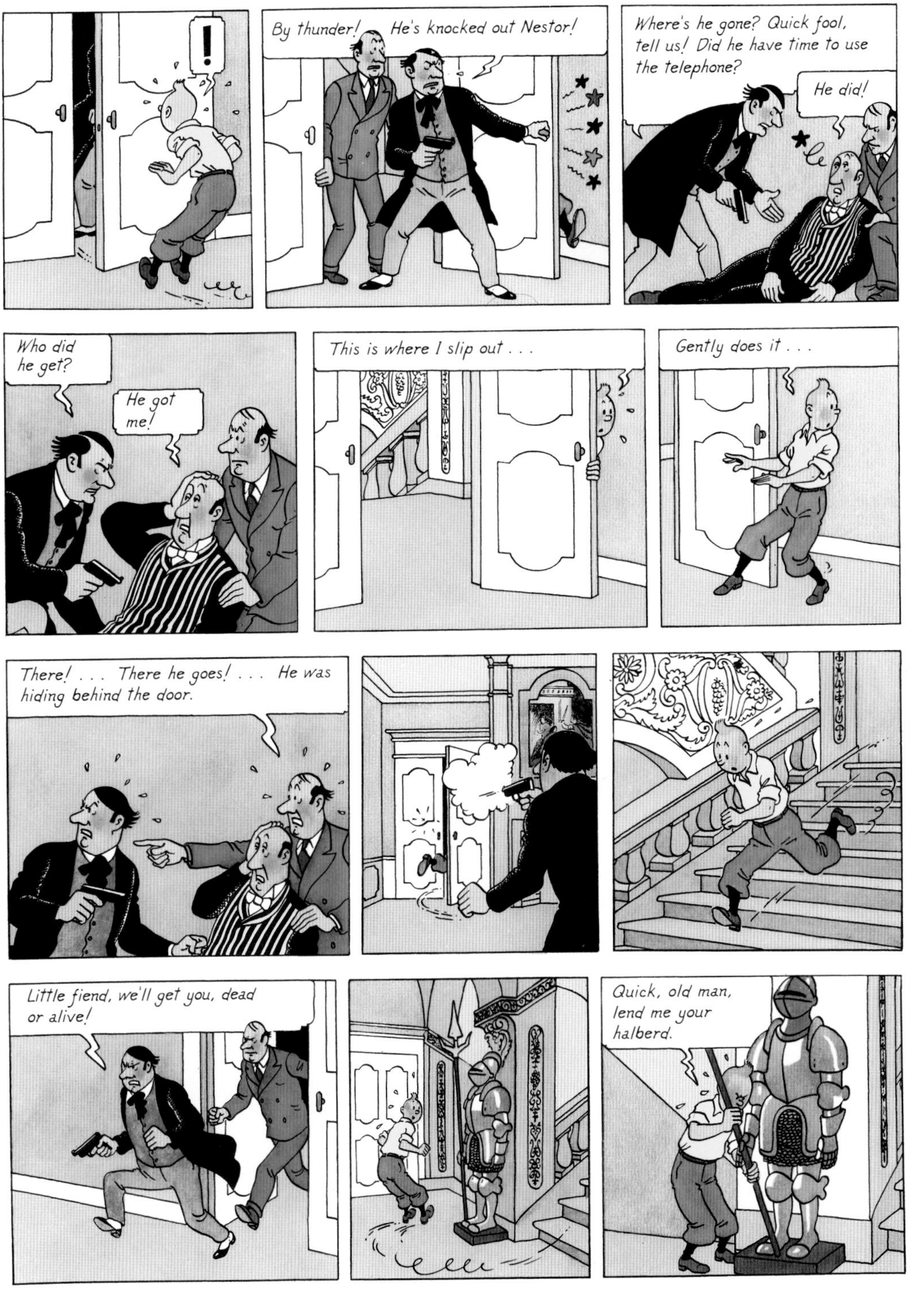
!
By thunder! He's knocked out Nestor!
Where's he gone? Quick fool, tell us! Did he have time to use the telephone?
He did!
Who did he get?
He got me!
This is where I slip out . . .
Gently does it . . .
There! . . . There he goes! . . . He was hiding behind the door.
Little fiend, we'll get you, dead or alive!
Quick, old man, lend me your halberd.

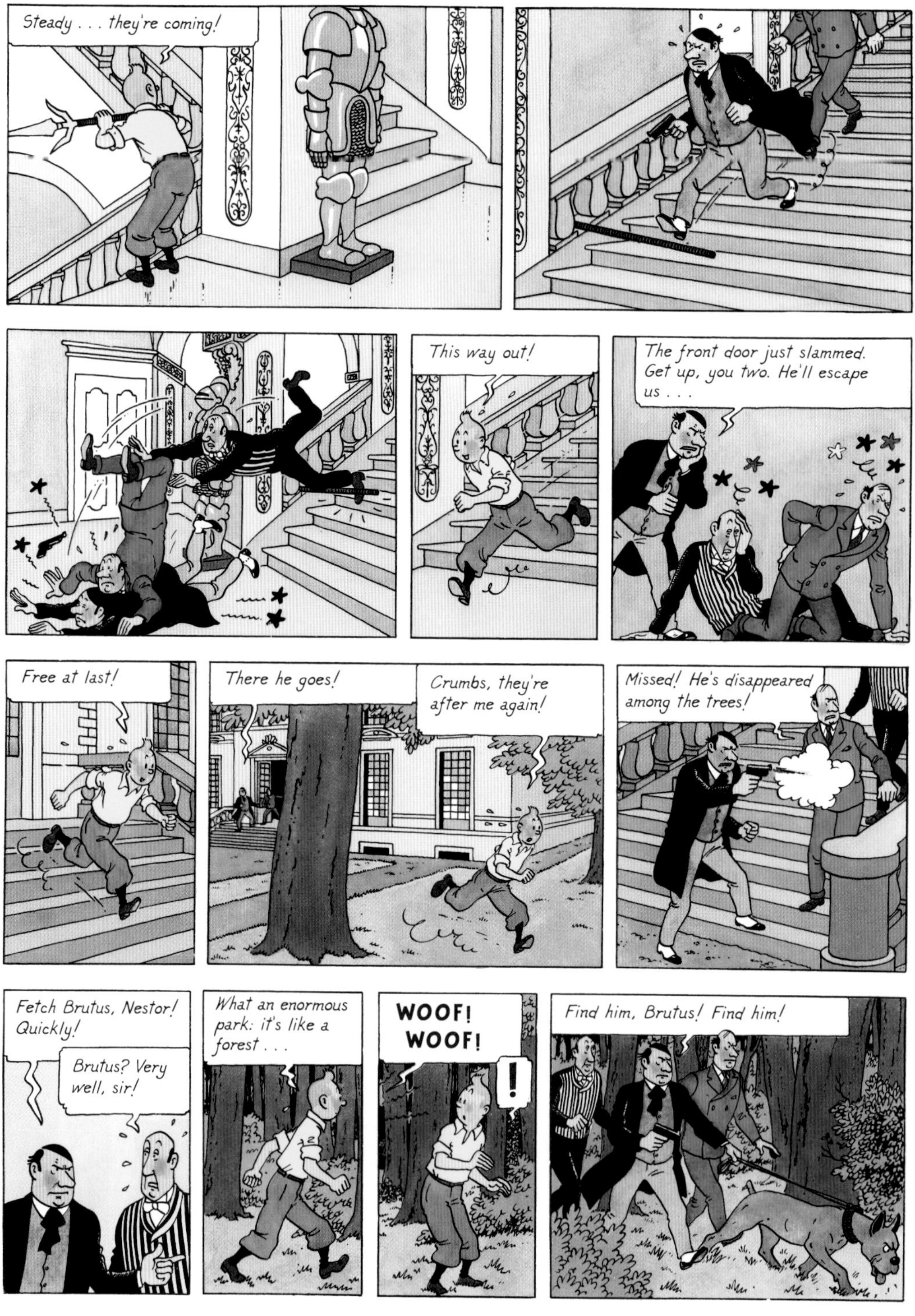
Steady . . . they're coming!
This way out!
The front door just slammed. Get up, you two. He'll escape us . . .
Free at last!
There he goes!
Crumbs, they're after me again!
Missed! He's disappeared among the trees!
Fetch Brutus, Nestor! Quickly!
Brutus? Very well, sir!
What an enormous park: it's like a forest . . .
WOOF! WOOF!
!
Find him, Brutus! Find him!

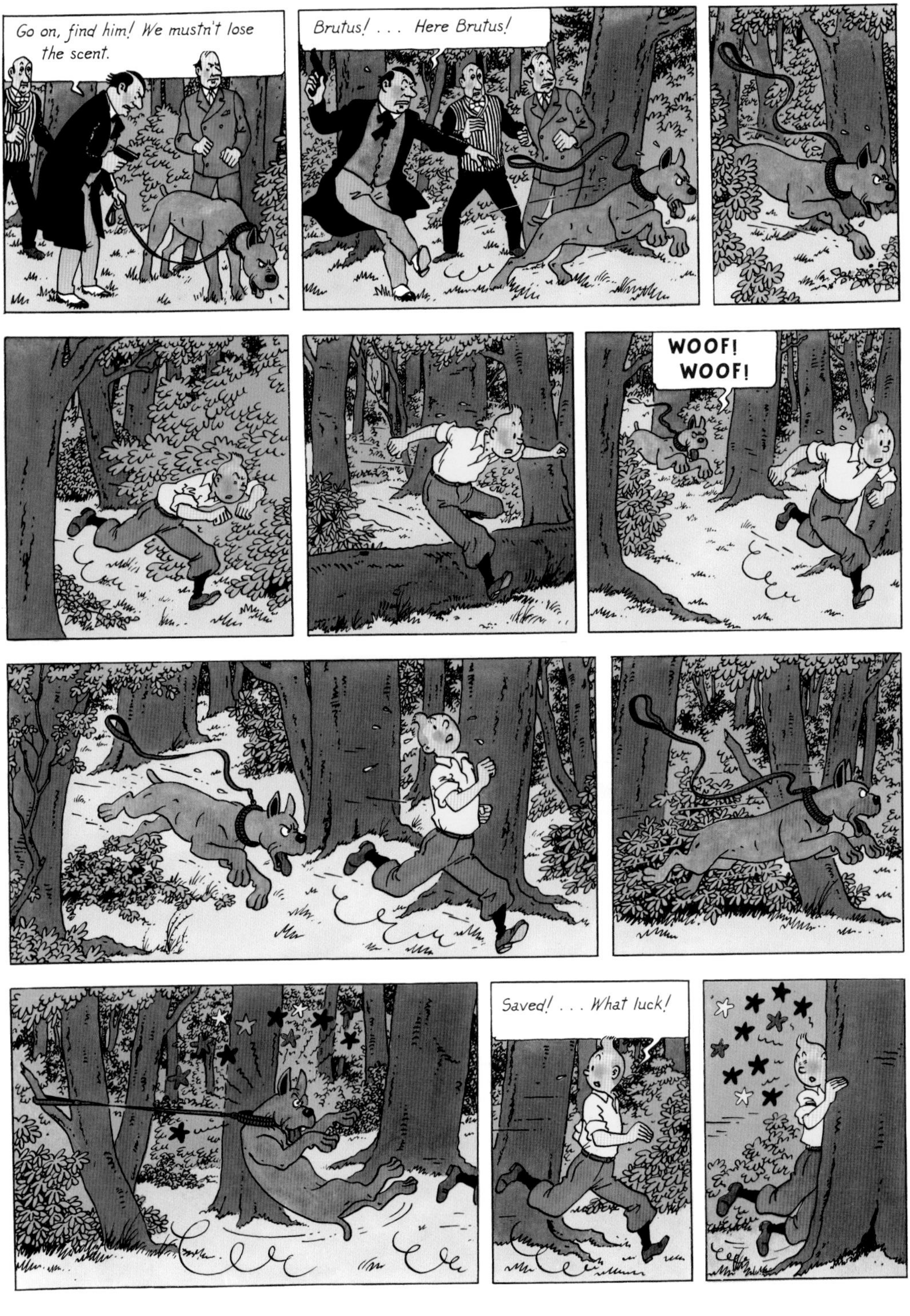
Go on, find him! We mustn't lose the scent.
Brutus! . . . Here Brutus!
WOOF! WOOF!
Saved! . . . What luck!

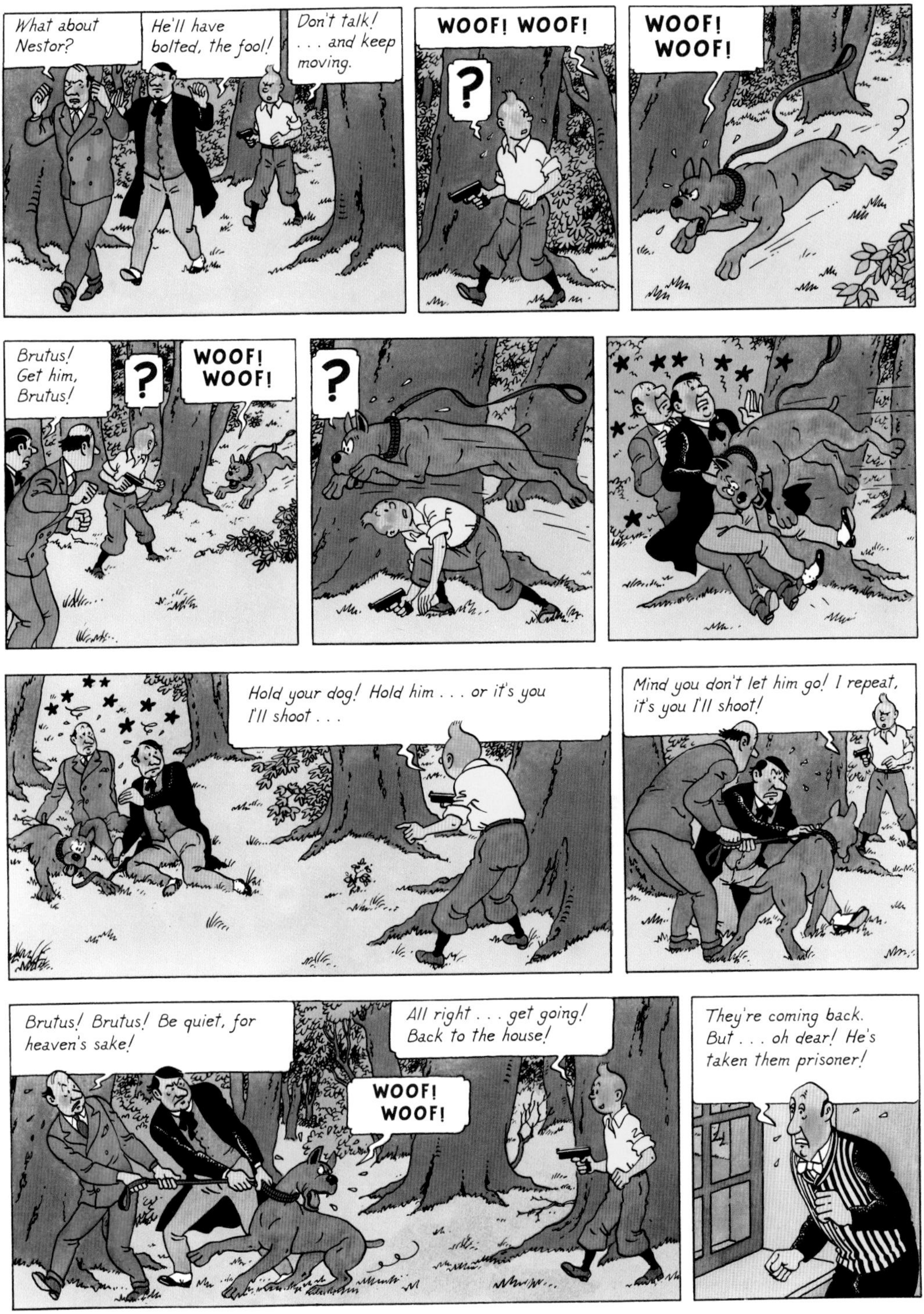
What about Nestor?
He'll have bolted, the fool!
Don't talk! . . . and keep moving.
WOOF! WOOF!
?
WOOF! WOOF!
Brutus! Get him, Brutus!
?
WOOF! WOOF!
?
Hold your dog! Hold him . . . or it's you I'll shoot . . .
Mind you don't let him go! I repeat, it's you I'll shoot!
Brutus! Brutus! Be quiet, for heaven's sake!
WOOF! WOOF!
All right . . . get going! Back to the house!
They're coming back. But . . . oh dear! He's taken them prisoner!

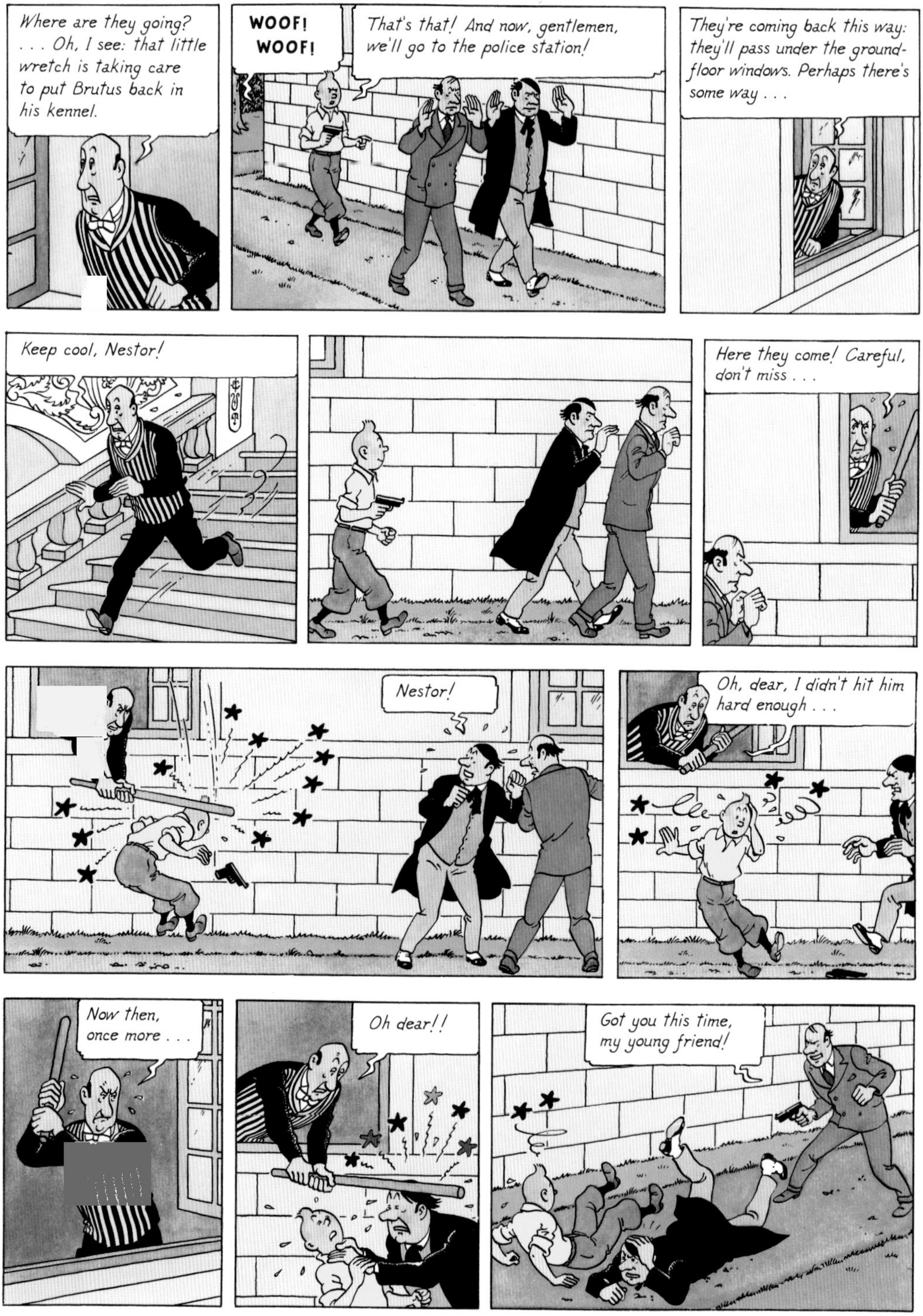
Where are they going? . . . Oh, I see: that little wretch is taking care to put Brutus back in his kennel.
WOOF! WOOF!
That's that! And now, gentlemen, we'll go to the police station!
They're coming back this way: they'll pass under the ground-floor windows. Perhaps there's some way . . .
Keep cool, Nestor!
Here they come! Careful, don't miss . . .
Nestor!
Oh, dear, I didn't hit him hard enough . . .
Now then, once more . . .
Oh dear!!
Got you this time, my young friend!

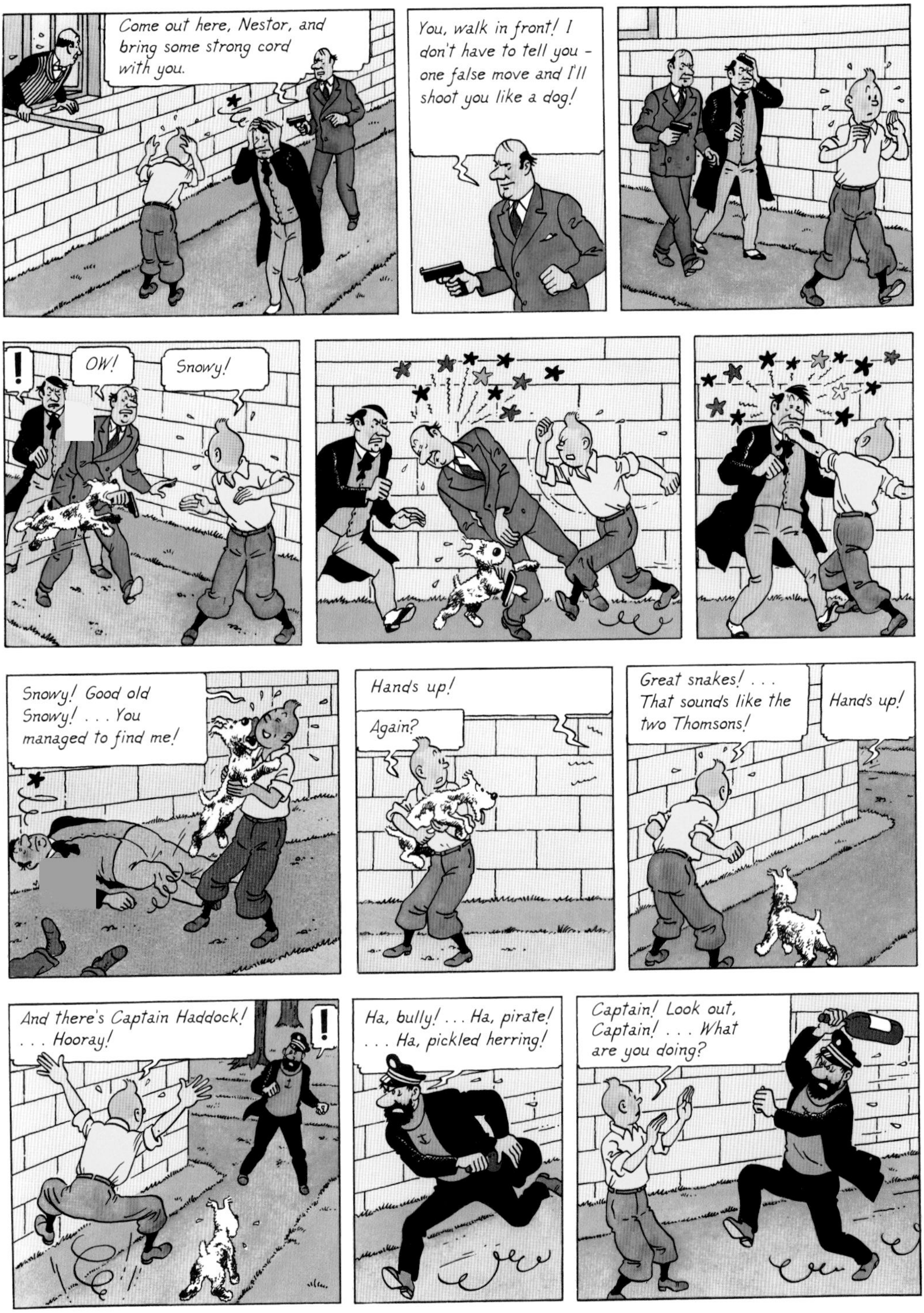
Come out here, Nestor, and bring some strong cord with you.
You, walk in front! I don't have to tell you - one false move and I'll shoot you like a dog!
!
OW!
Snowy!
Snowy! Good old Snowy! . . . You managed to find me!
Hands up!
Again?
Great snakes! . . . That sounds like the two Thomsons!
Hands up!
And there's Captain Haddock! . . . Hooray!
!
Ha, bully! . . . Ha, pirate! . . . Ha, pickled herring!
Captain! Look out, Captain! . . . What are you doing?

That's one for you, sycophant!

That thug had come round – he was just going to shoot you . . .

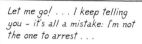

Let me go! . . . I keep telling you – it's all a mistake: I'm not the one to arrest . . .

Ah, here come Thomson and Thompson . . . Hello.

It's this little ruffian, this little wretch who broke into the house and terrorized my masters; he's a real gangster, Mr Detective . . .

It's true, Nestor acted in good faith. I heard his master say I was a criminal. Nestor believed it.

Then your masters are the criminals. Look what's left of my bottle of three-star brandy! It's all their fault! . . . They're gangsters! . . . dizzards! baboons!

And what's more, we have a warrant for their arrest.

My wallet! My wallet! It's incredible!

But your wallet's there . . .

That's just what's incredible: no one has stolen it!

By the way, what about that pickpocket? . . . Have you managed to lay hands on him?

Not yet, but it won't be long now.

We got his name from the Stellar Cleaners: he's called Aristides Silk. We were just about to pull him in when we were ordered to arrest the Bird brothers, and here we are . . .

Quiet! Quiet! Listen to me!

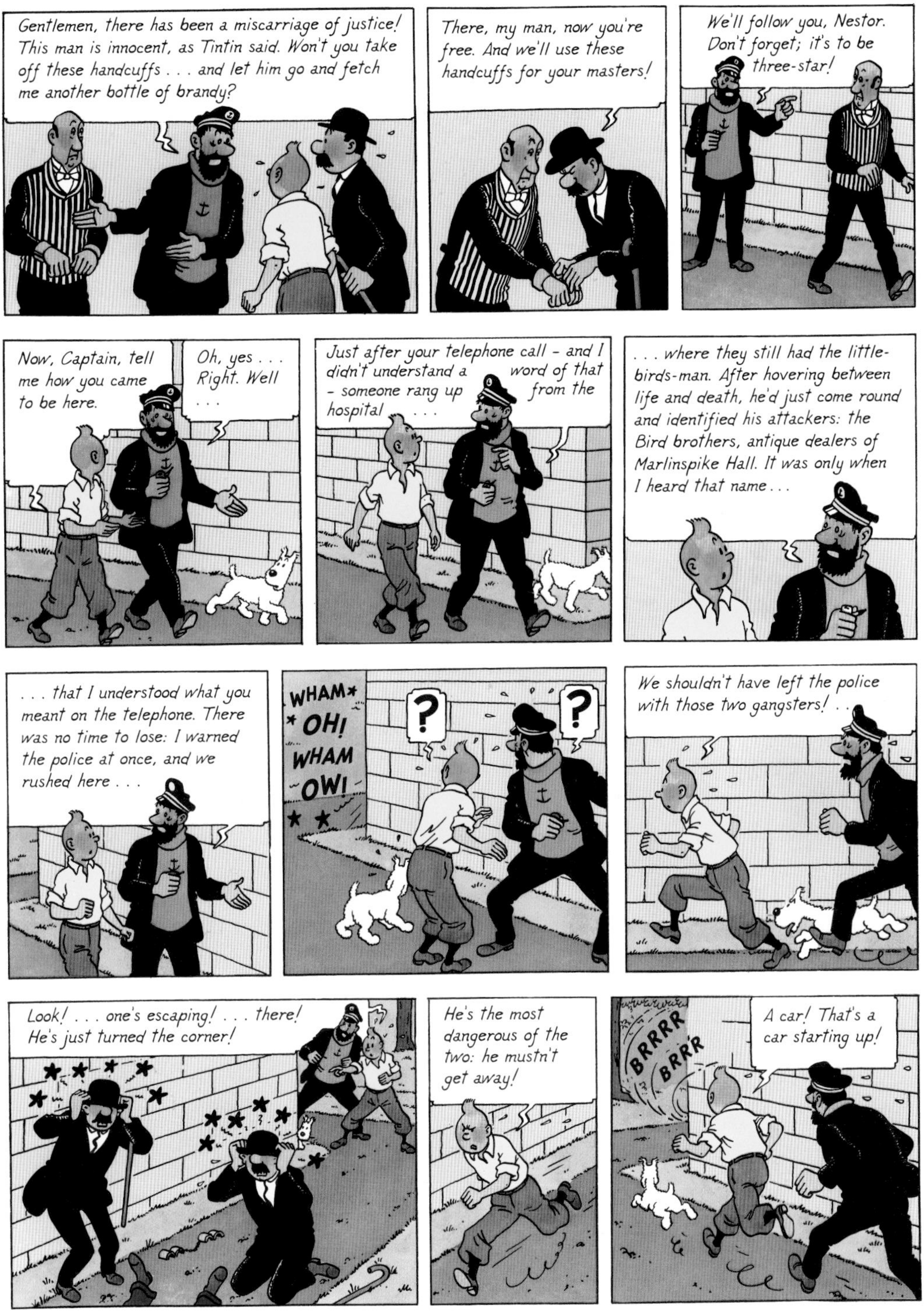
Gentlemen, there has been a miscarriage of justice! This man is innocent, as Tintin said. Won't you take off these handcuffs . . . and let him go and fetch me another bottle of brandy?
There, my man, now you're free. And we'll use these handcuffs for your masters!
We'll follow you, Nestor. Don't forget; it's to be three-star!
Now, Captain, tell me how you came to be here.
Oh, yes . . . Right. Well . . .
Just after your telephone call - and I didn't understand a word of that - someone rang up from the hospital . . .
. . . where they still had the little-birds-man. After hovering between life and death, he'd just come round and identified his attackers: the Bird brothers, antique dealers of Marlinspike Hall. It was only when I heard that name . . .
. . . that I understood what you meant on the telephone. There was no time to lose: I warned the police at once, and we rushed here . . .
WHAM
OH!
WHAM
OW!
?
?
We shouldn't have left the police with those two gangsters! . . .
Look! . . . one's escaping! . . . there! He's just turned the corner!
He's the most dangerous of the two: he mustn't get away!
BRRRR
BRRR
A car! That's a car starting up!

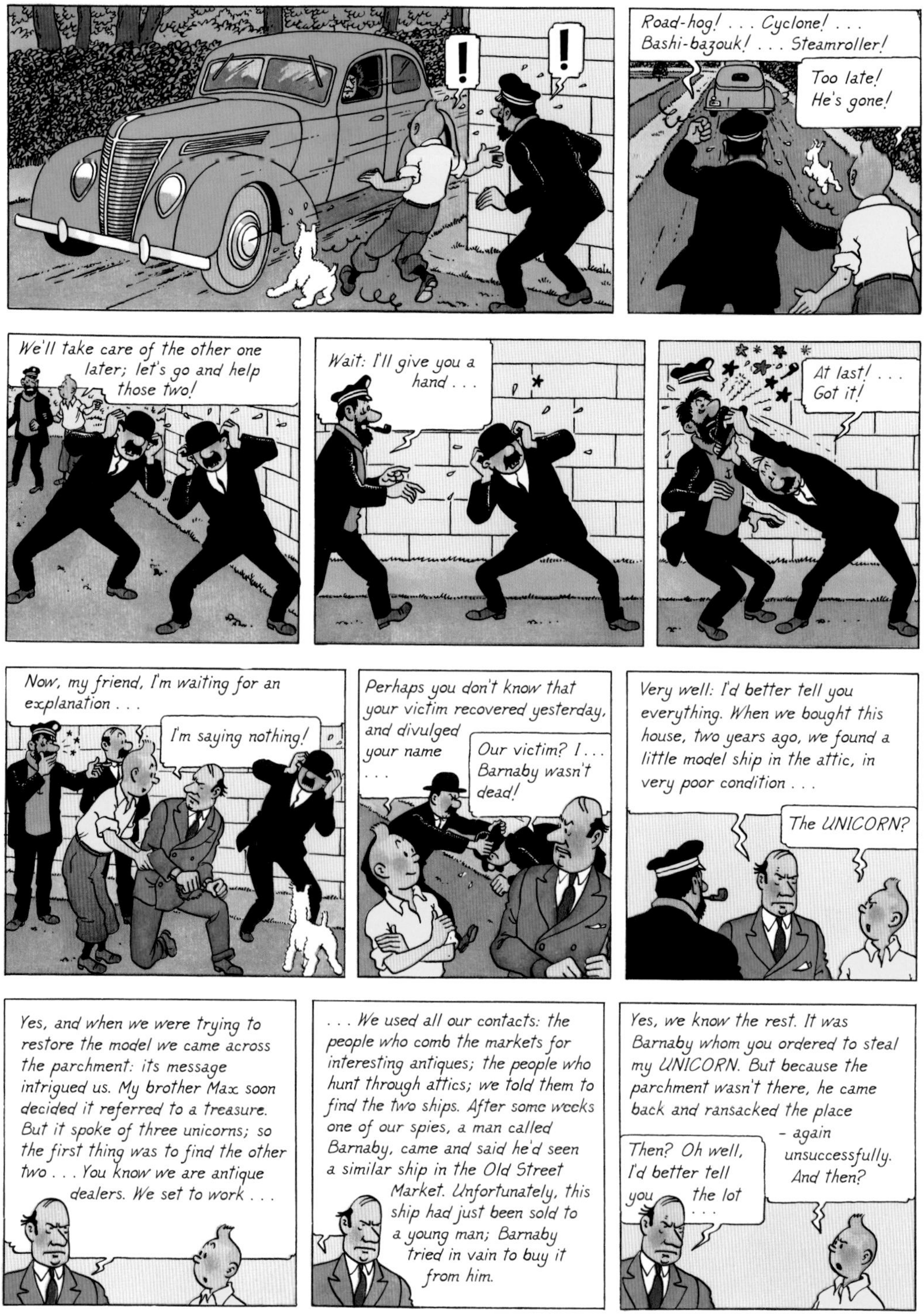
!
!
Road-hog! . . . Cyclone! . . . Bashi-bazouk! . . . Steamroller!
Too late! He's gone!
We'll take care of the other one later; let's go and help those two!
Wait: I'll give you a hand . . .
At last! . . . Got it!
Now, my friend, I'm waiting for an explanation . . .
I'm saying nothing!
Perhaps you don't know that your victim recovered yesterday, and divulged your name . . .
Our victim? I . . . Barnaby wasn't dead!
Very well: I'd better tell you everything. When we bought this house, two years ago, we found a little model ship in the attic, in very poor condition . . .
The UNICORN?
Yes, and when we were trying to restore the model we came across the parchment: its message intrigued us. My brother Max soon decided it referred to a treasure. But it spoke of three unicorns; so the first thing was to find the other two . . . You know we are antique dealers. We set to work . . .
. . . We used all our contacts: the people who comb the markets for interesting antiques; the people who hunt through attics; we told them to find the two ships. After some weeks one of our spies, a man called Barnaby, came and said he'd seen a similar ship in the Old Street Market. Unfortunately, this ship had just been sold to a young man; Barnaby tried in vain to buy it from him.
Yes, we know the rest. It was Barnaby whom you ordered to steal my UNICORN. But because the parchment wasn't there, he came back and ransacked the place – again unsuccessfully. And then?
Then? Oh well, I'd better tell you the lot . . .

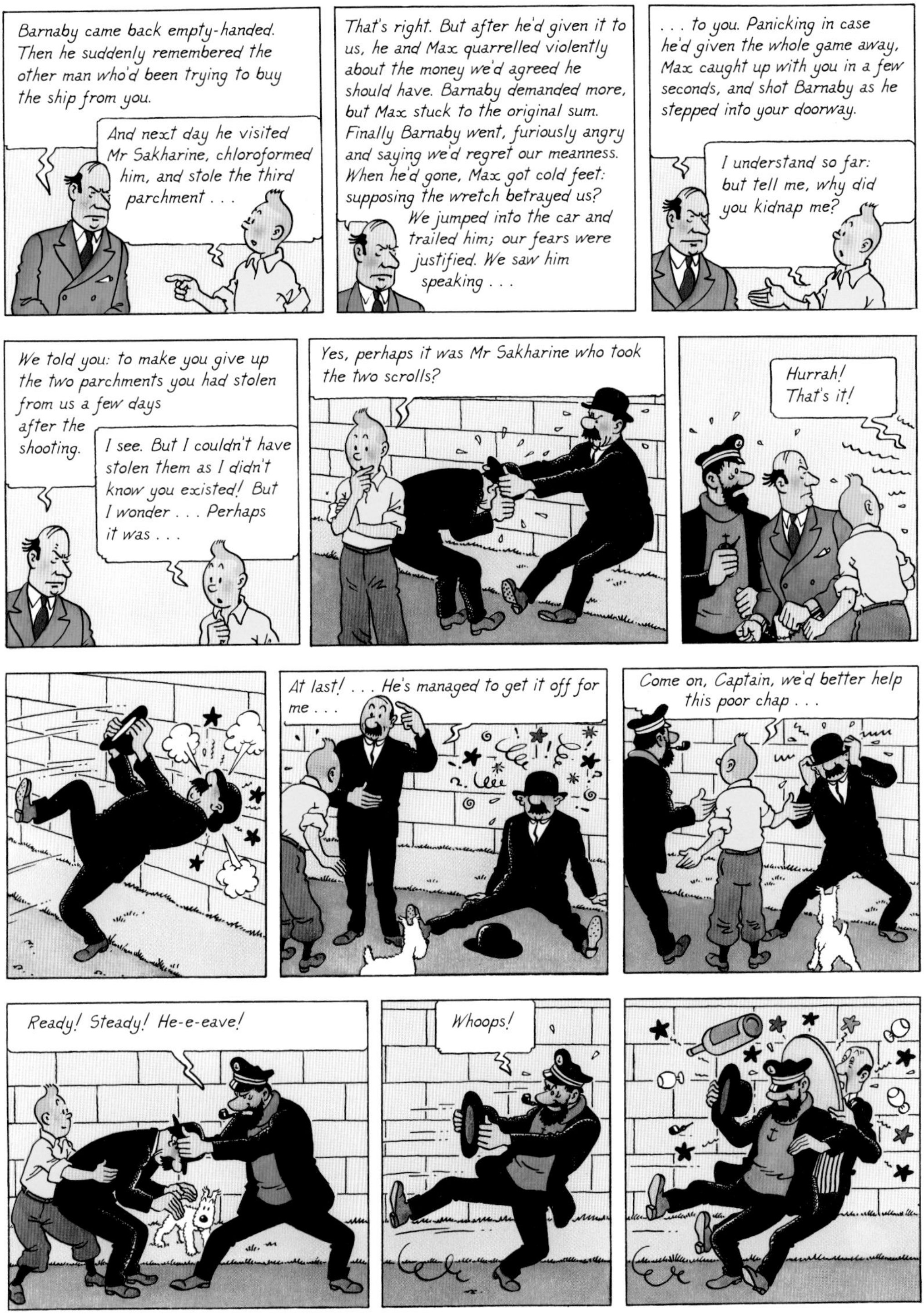

Barnaby came back empty-handed. Then he suddenly remembered the other man who'd been trying to buy the ship from you.
And next day he visited Mr Sakharine, chloroformed him, and stole the third parchment . . .
That's right. But after he'd given it to us, he and Max quarrelled violently about the money we'd agreed he should have. Barnaby demanded more, but Max stuck to the original sum. Finally Barnaby went, furiously angry and saying we'd regret our meanness. When he'd gone, Max got cold feet: supposing the wretch betrayed us?
We jumped into the car and trailed him; our fears were justified. We saw him speaking . . .
. . . to you. Panicking in case he'd given the whole game away, Max caught up with you in a few seconds, and shot Barnaby as he stepped into your doorway.
I understand so far: but tell me, why did you kidnap me?
We told you: to make you give up the two parchments you had stolen from us a few days after the shooting.
I see. But I couldn't have stolen them as I didn't know you existed! But I wonder . . . Perhaps it was . . .
Yes, perhaps it was Mr Sakharine who took the two scrolls?
Hurrah! That's it!
At last! . . . He's managed to get it off for me . . .
Come on, Captain, we'd better help this poor chap . . .
Ready! Steady! He-e-eave!
Whoops!

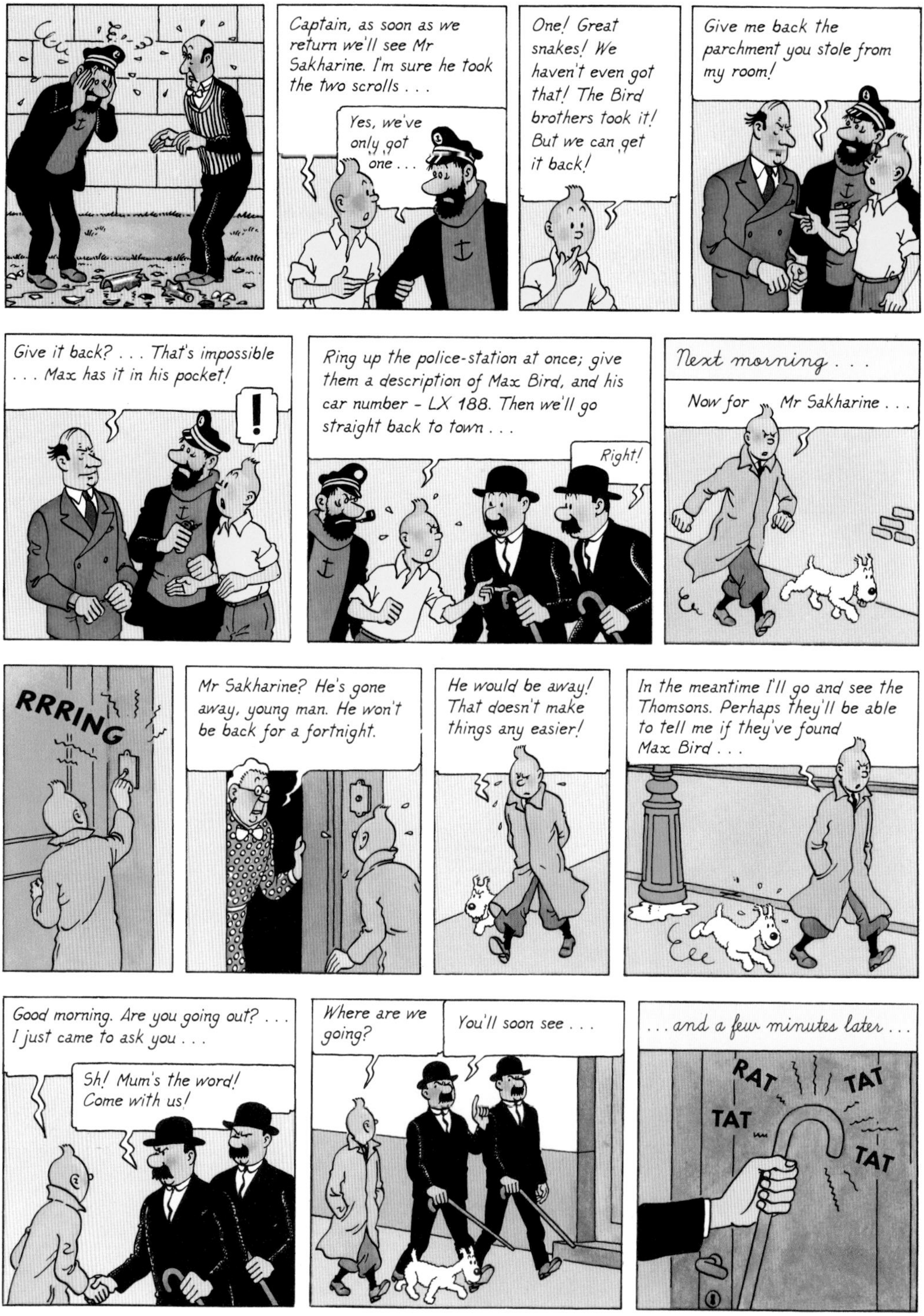
Captain, as soon as we return we'll see Mr Sakharine. I'm sure he took the two scrolls . . .
Yes, we've only got one . . .
One! Great snakes! We haven't even got that! The Bird brothers took it! But we can get it back!
Give me back the parchment you stole from my room!
Give it back? . . . That's impossible . . . Max has it in his pocket!
!
Ring up the police-station at once; give them a description of Max Bird, and his car number - LX 188. Then we'll go straight back to town . . .
Right!
Next morning . . .
Now for Mr Sakharine . . .
RRRING
Mr Sakharine? He's gone away, young man. He won't be back for a fortnight.
He would be away! That doesn't make things any easier!
In the meantime I'll go and see the Thomsons. Perhaps they'll be able to tell me if they've found Max Bird . . .
Good morning. Are you going out? . . . I just came to ask you . . .
Sh! Mum's the word! Come with us!
Where are we going?
You'll soon see . . .
. . . and a few minutes later . . .
RAT TAT TAT TAT

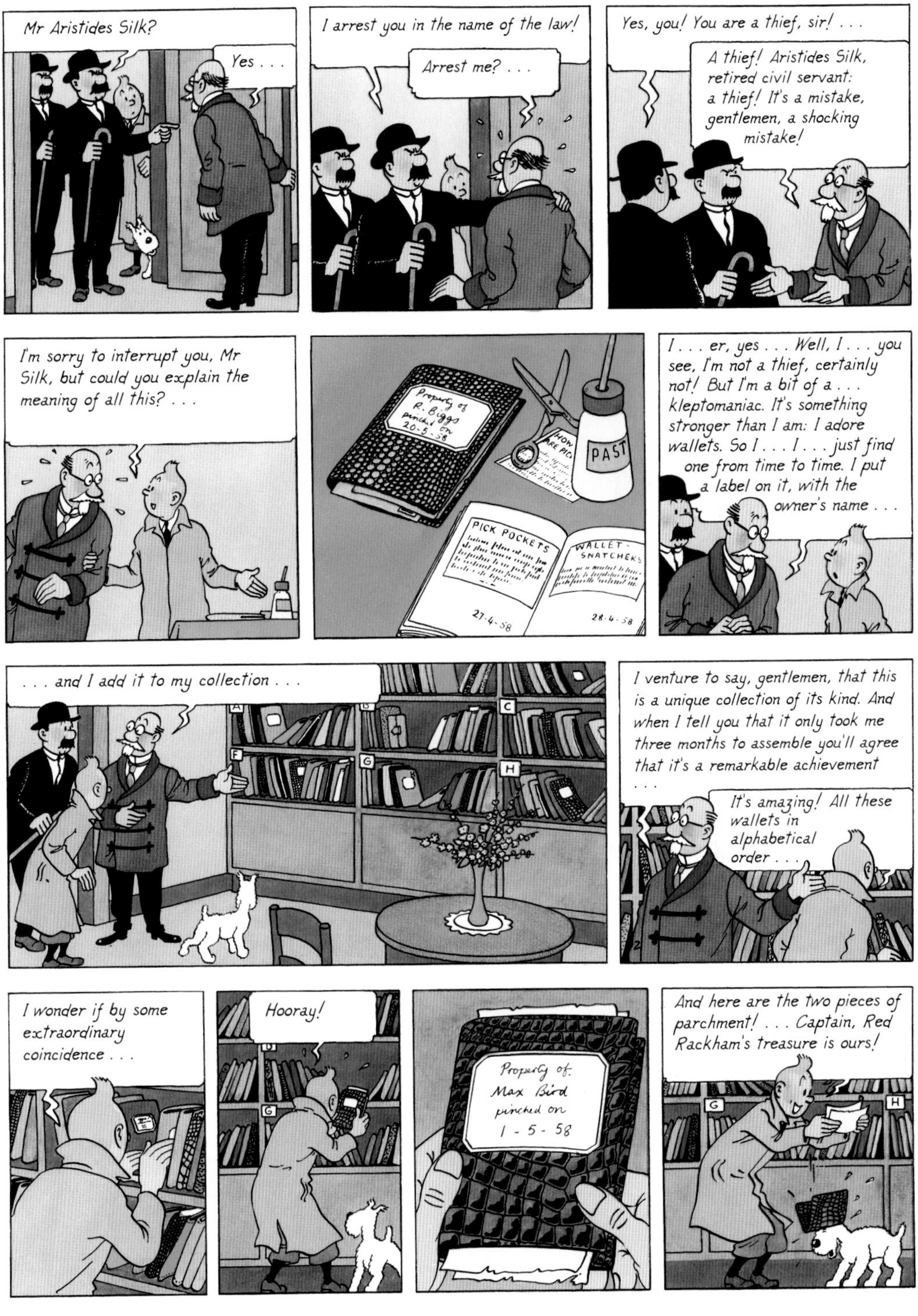
Mr Aristides Silk?
Yes . . .
I arrest you in the name of the law!
Arrest me? . . .
Yes, you! You are a thief, sir! . . .
A thief! Aristides Silk, retired civil servant: a thief! It's a mistake, gentlemen, a shocking mistake!
I'm sorry to interrupt you, Mr Silk, but could you explain the meaning of all this? . . .
Property of R. Biggs pinched on 20-5-58
PAST
PICK POCKETS
WALLET-SNATCHERS
27-4-58
28-4-58
I . . . er, yes . . . Well, I . . . you see, I'm not a thief, certainly not! But I'm a bit of a . . . kleptomaniac. It's something stronger than I am: I adore wallets. So I . . . I . . . just find one from time to time. I put a label on it, with the owner's name . . .
. . . and I add it to my collection . . .
A
C
F
G
H
I venture to say, gentlemen, that this is a unique collection of its kind. And when I tell you that it only took me three months to assemble you'll agree that it's a remarkable achievement . . .
It's amazing! All these wallets in alphabetical order . . .
I wonder if by some extraordinary coincidence . . .
Hooray!
G
Property of Max Bird pinched on 1 - 5 - 58
And here are the two pieces of parchment! . . . Captain, Red Rackham's treasure is ours!
G
H

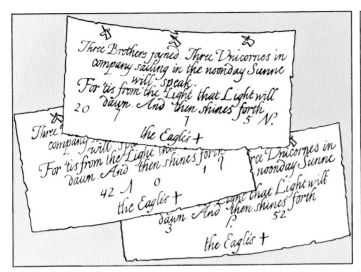

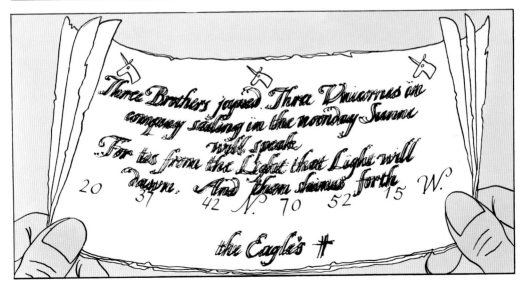

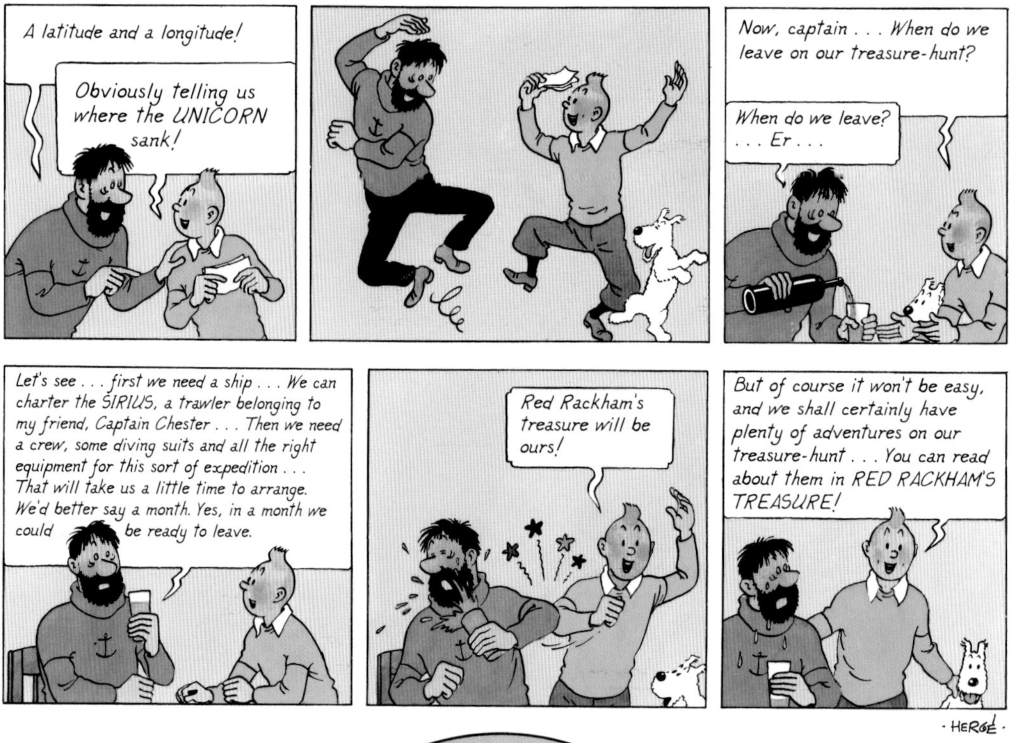
A latitude and a longitude!
Obviously telling us where the UNICORN sank!
Now, captain . . . When do we leave on our treasure-hunt?
When do we leave? . . . Er . . .
Let's see . . . first we need a ship . . . We can charter the SIRIUS, a trawler belonging to my friend, Captain Chester . . . Then we need a crew, some diving suits and all the right equipment for this sort of expedition . . . That will take us a little time to arrange. We'd better say a month. Yes, in a month we could be ready to leave.
Red Rackham's treasure will be ours!
But of course it won't be easy, and we shall certainly have plenty of adventures on our treasure-hunt . . . You can read about them in RED RACKHAM'S TREASURE!
· HERGÉ ·

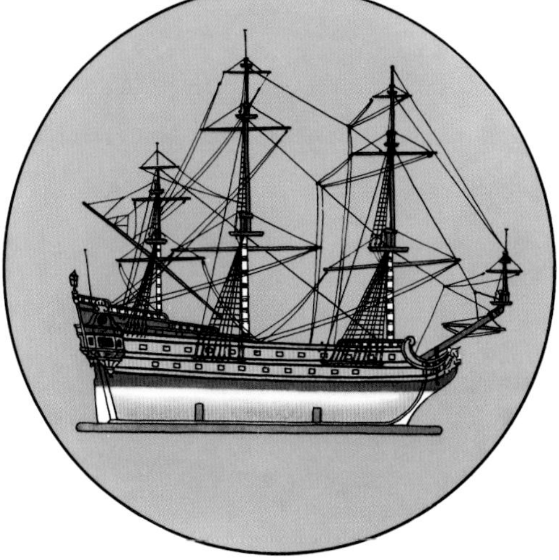

THE REAL-LIFE INSPIRATION BEHIND TINTIN'S ADVENTURES

Written by Stuart Tett
with the collaboration of Dominique Maricq and Studio Moulinsart.

GEORGES REMI BORN IN BELGIUM
1907

CHOOSES PEN-NAME "HERGÉ" – HIS INITIALS "G.R." REVERSED
1924

HERGÉ LEAVES SCHOOL
1925

HERGÉ HELPS TO CREATE CHILDREN'S MAGAZINE: *LE PETIT VINGTIÈME*
1928

TINTIN'S FIRST ADVENTURE, *TINTIN IN THE LAND OF THE SOVIETS*, APPEARS IN *LE PETIT VINGTIÈME*
1929

HERGÉ

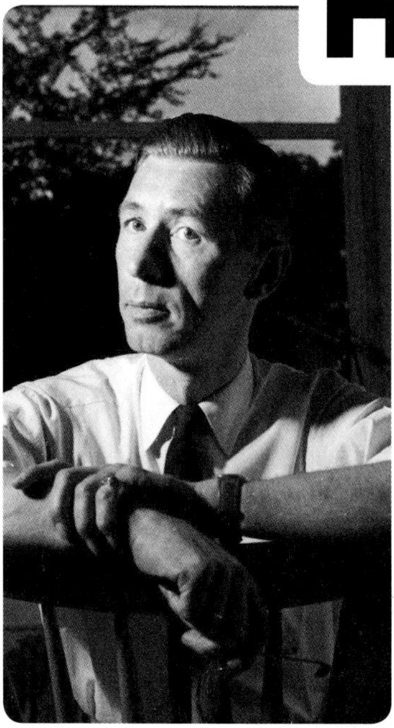

Coloring Tintin

Every time that Hergé wrote a Tintin story, it was first published as comic strips in a newspaper or magazine, and later collected into a book. Initially, Hergé drew all of Tintin's adventures in black and white.

In 1942, Casterman, the publisher of the Tintin books, decided that the books should be in color, and should be 62 pages long. Casterman asked Hergé to redraw eight of the existing Tintin adventures to fit into the new format.

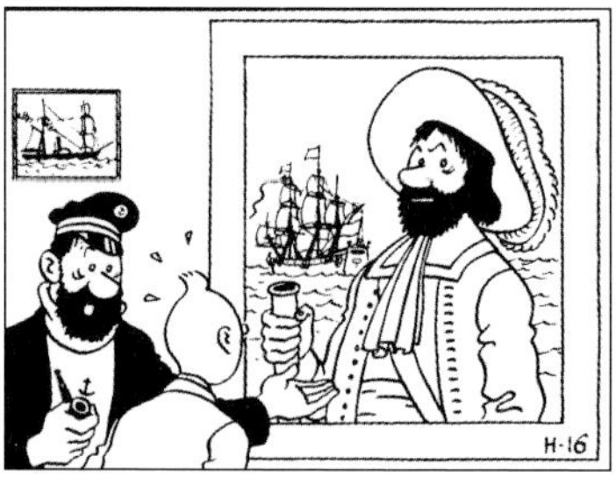
H-16

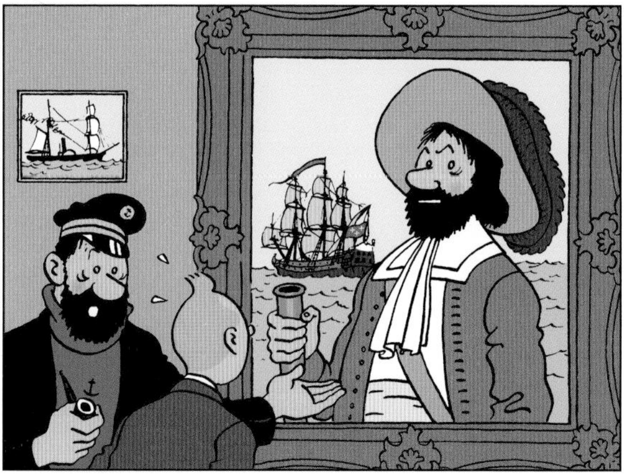

PUBLICATION OF *THE SECRET OF THE UNICORN*	LAUNCH OF *TINTIN* MAGAZINE	HERGÉ VISITS AMERICA	PUBLICATION OF TINTIN'S LAST ADVENTURE, *TINTIN AND THE PICAROS*	HERGÉ DIES AGED 75
1943	**1946**	**1971**	**1976**	**1983**

TINTIN

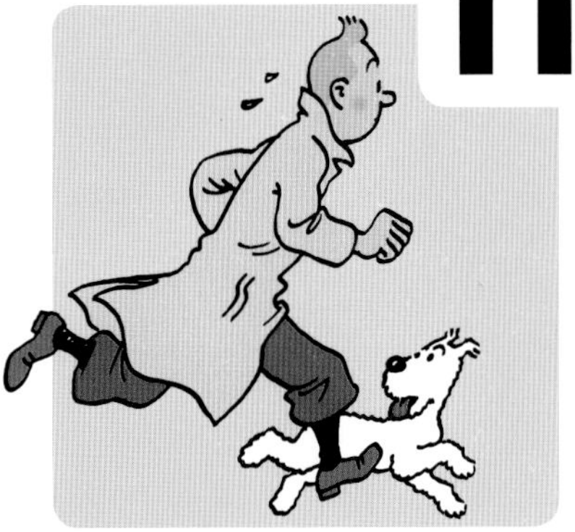

At the movies

In 1961 and 1964, two live-action movies were made about Tintin. Several decades later, Steven Spielberg used motion capture technology to create the 2011 film *The Adventures of Tintin: Secret of the Unicorn*!

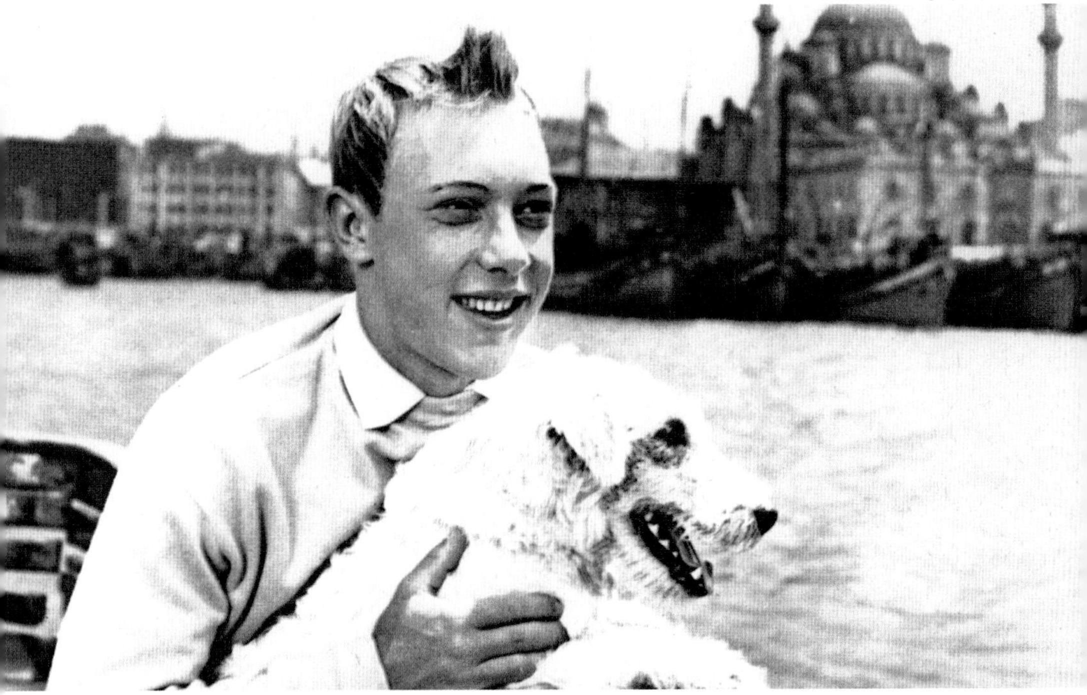

Jean-Pierre Talbot – *Tintin and the Golden Fleece*

THE TRUE STORY

… behind *The Secret of the Unicorn*

The first scene of the story is taken straight from the life of a Belgian citizen. In Brussels, the capital city of Belgium, there is a market held every day. Here is a photo of Hergé at the market. Who does he remind you of?

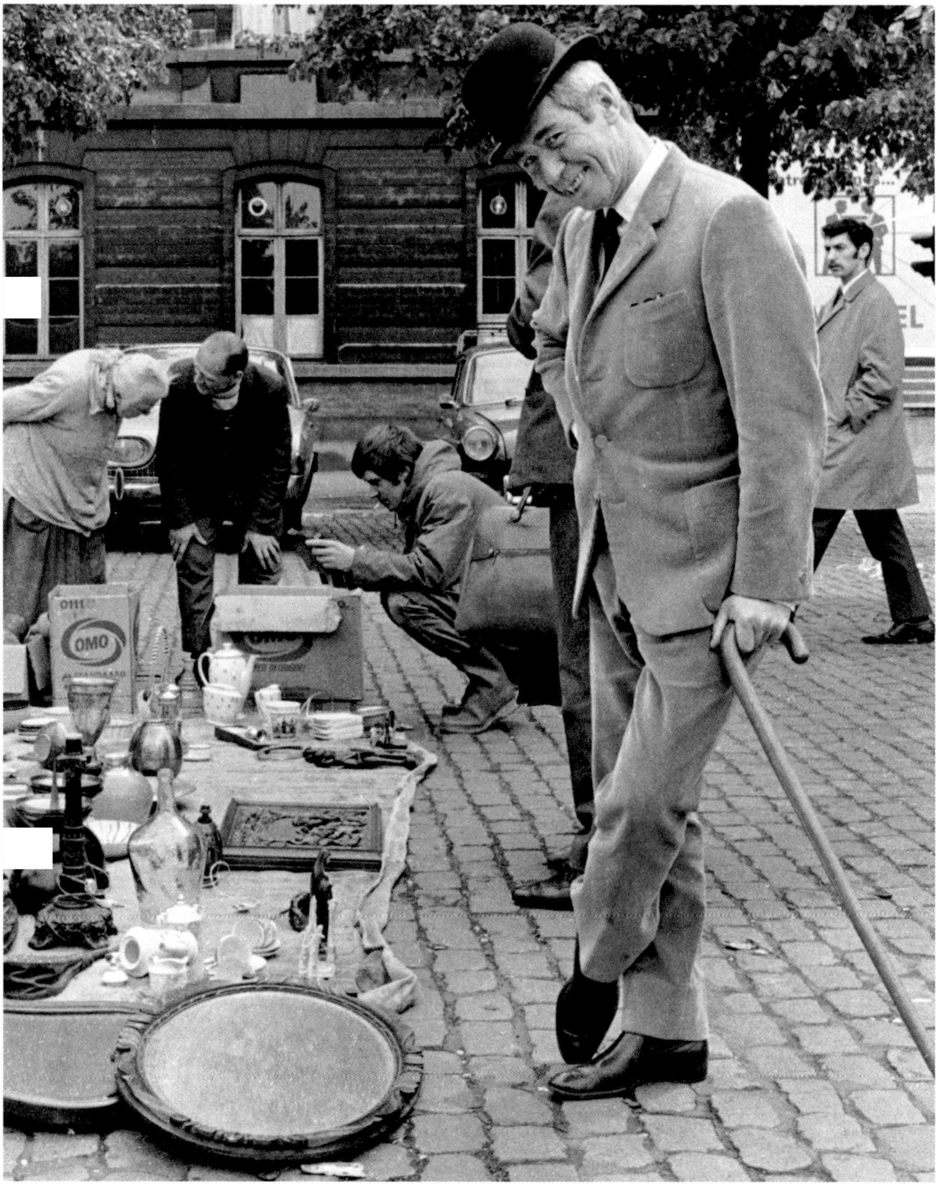
OMO

At the market, Tintin and the Thom(p)sons do a bit of shopping. The value of money has changed a lot since the early 1940s. The Thom(p)sons pay 7 shillings (known as 7 "bob") for their walking sticks, which today is worth about $15. Tintin buys his ship for 17 shillings and sixpence: $40 today.

In the story, when Tintin leaves the market he is hounded by two mysterious men who want to buy his model ship. In today's money they start offering him $100s: the last offer of £30 is today worth $1,350! If you bought a friend a present for $40 and then someone offered you over $1,000 for it, would you be able to say "no"?

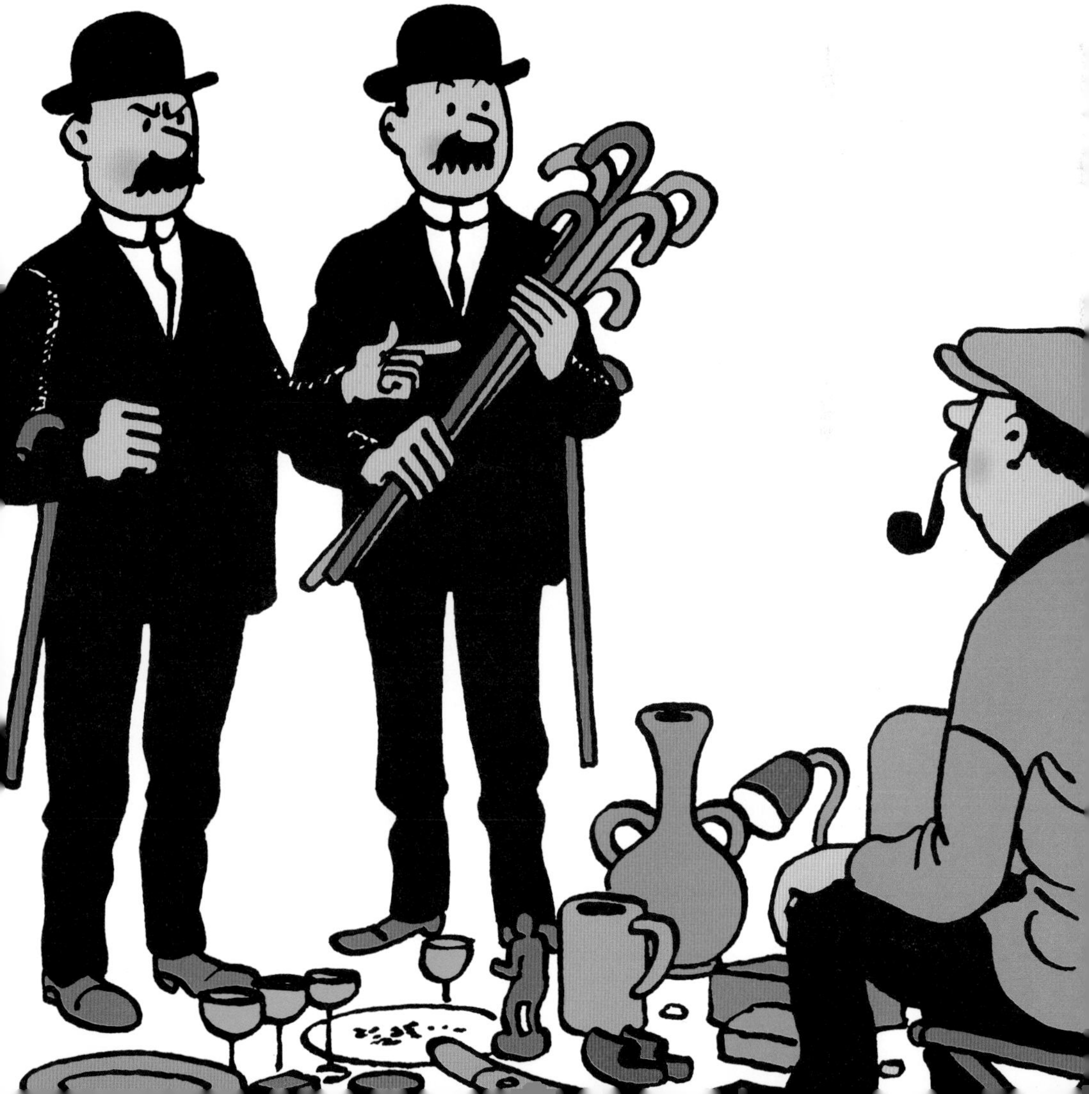

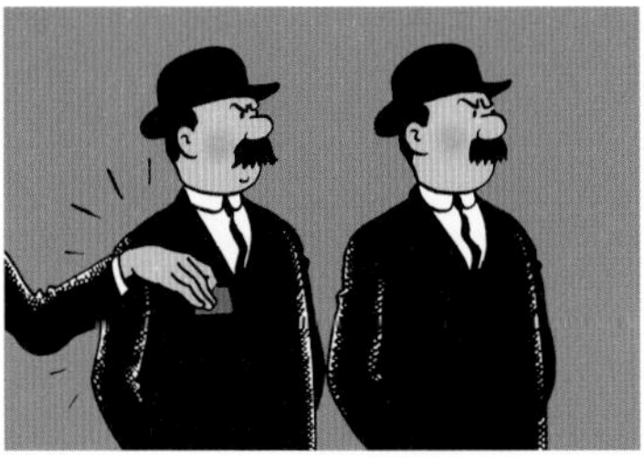

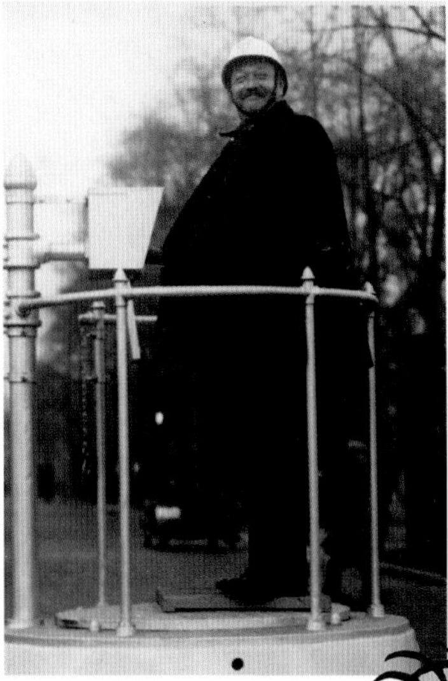

Once upon a time...

Hergé wrote *The Secret of the Unicorn* in 1942. Europe was at war and people struggled to earn a living. Brussels daily newspapers reported a certain type of crime: petty theft!

Pickpockets were working overtime! Hergé was inspired by this news when he created Aristides Silk, a pickpocket who keeps the Thom(p)sons very busy. Before the bumbling detectives manage to arrest the elusive Mr. Silk, they even get mistaken for thieves themselves! Hergé drew the Belgian policeman with an authentic uniform, as you can see from the picture on the left.

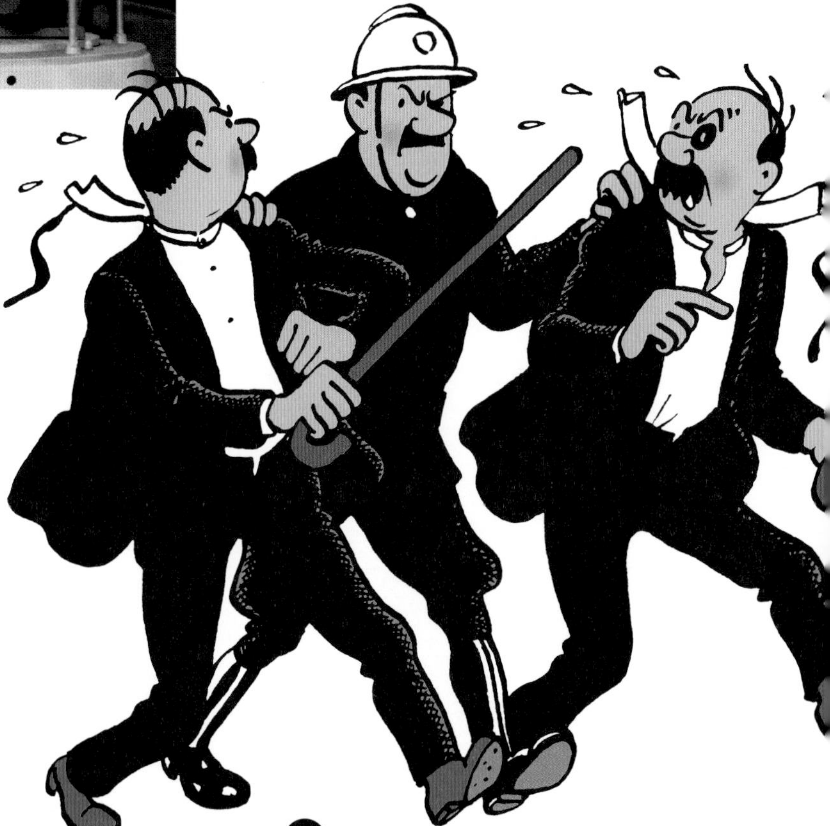

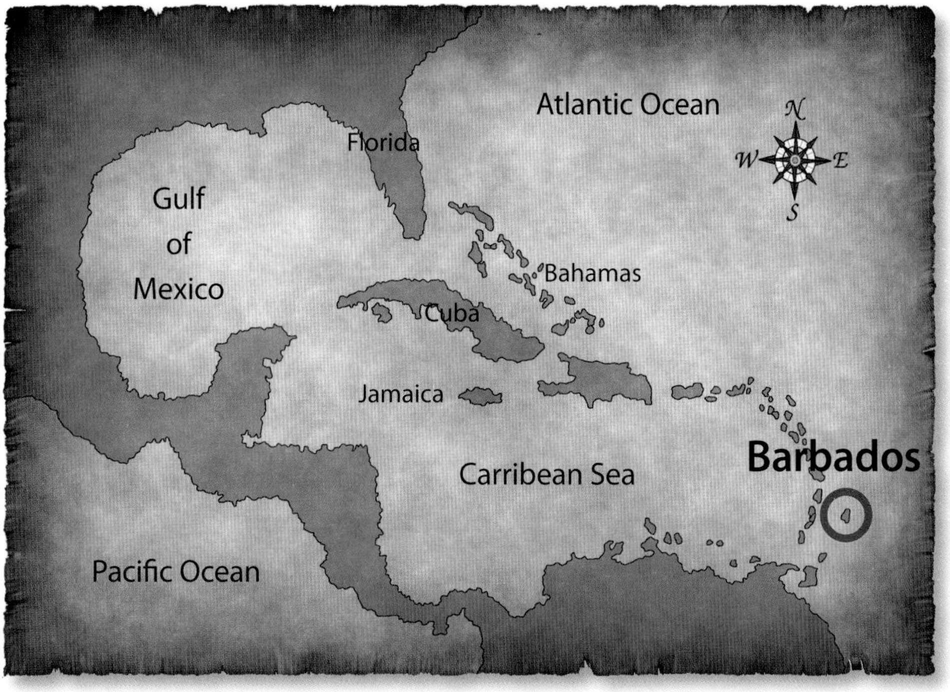
Atlantic Ocean
N
W
E
S
Florida
Gulf
of
Mexico
Bahamas
Cuba
Jamaica
Barbados
Carribean Sea
Pacific Ocean

In the story, the little ship from the market is a model of a real ship – the *Unicorn*. The real *Unicorn* is the key to the story of Sir Francis Haddock. The ship set sail from Barbados in 1676. At that time, Barbados was the world's biggest exporter of sugar, but what cargo was the *Unicorn* carrying? There is no mention of sugar, and Captain Haddock only confirms "a good deal of rum aboard." Perhaps the *Unicorn* is a warship?

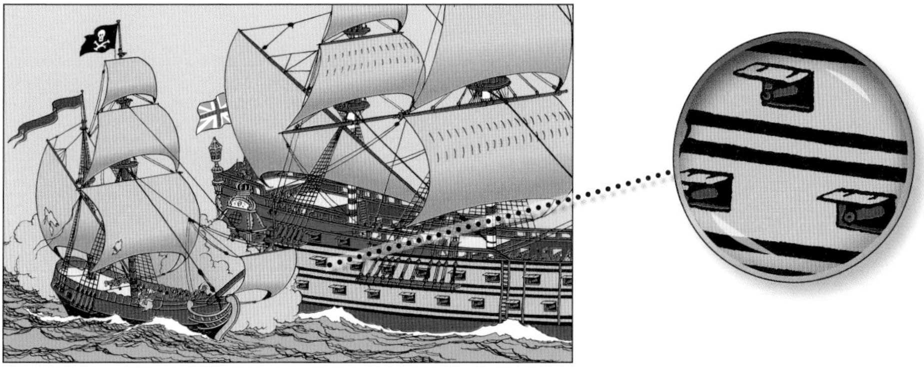

If you look carefully you will see that the *Unicorn* has roughly 50 cannons, so it looks like it is a ship made for fighting after all!

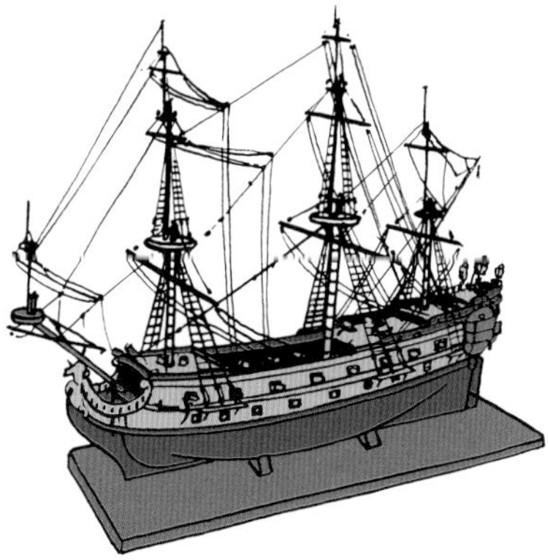

When Captain Haddock has finished recounting the tale of his ancestor, Tintin suddenly realizes that Sir Francis Haddock hid instructions leading to Red Rackham's treasure inside the masts of three little model ships. He also realizes that he already has one of the ships... it is the model he bought from the market!

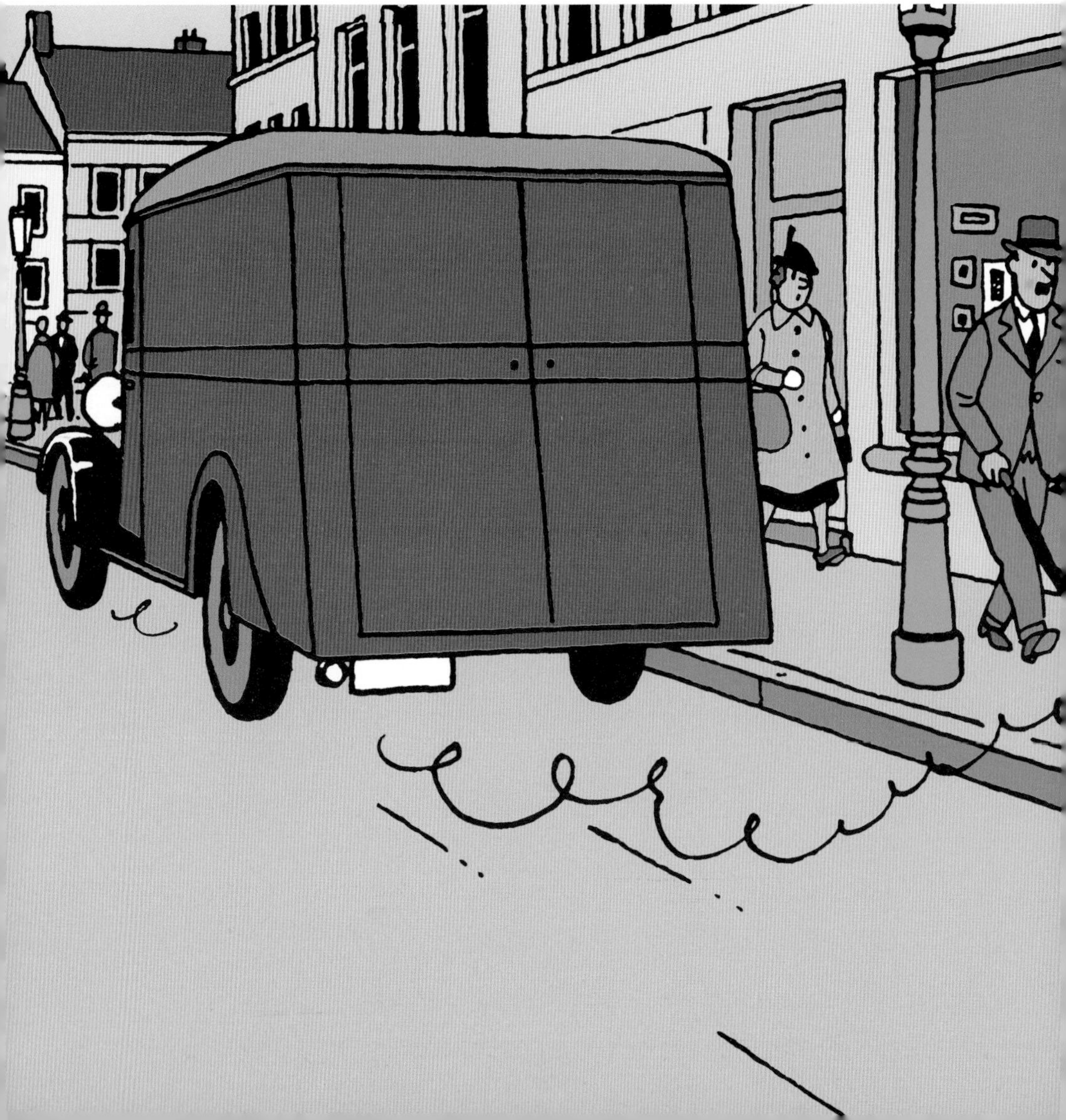

Once upon a time...

From this point onward, the story carries on in the 1940s. This was during World War II. In Belgium, German troops imposed strict control over the gasoline supply, which meant that not many people could afford to drive cars. Hergé reflected this reality in his story. Apart from the red van, how many other vehicles do you see in this book?

We have just been looking at the real-life stories behind Tintin's adventure. Now it's time to **Explore and Discover!**

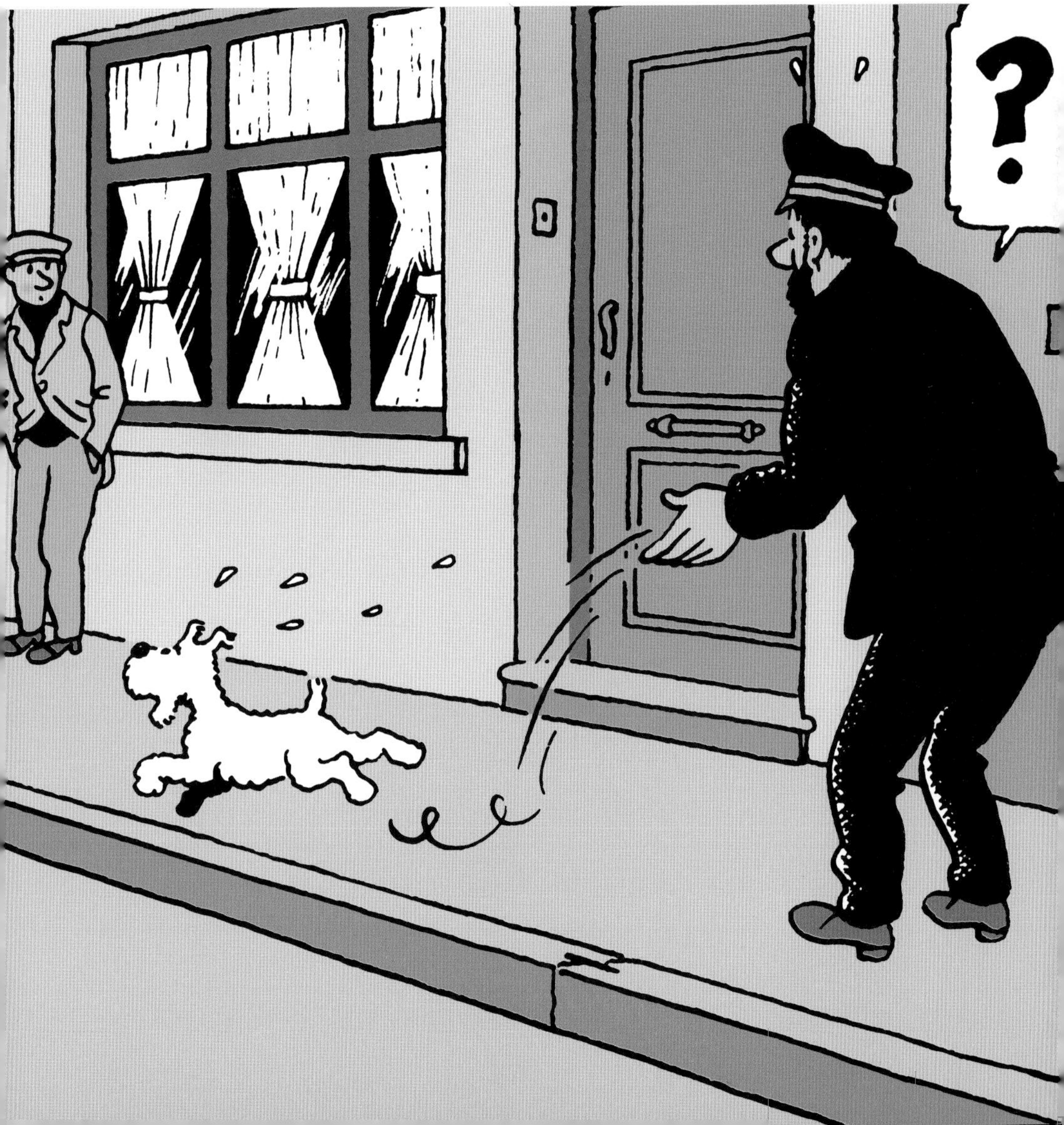
?

EXPLORE AND DISCOVER

Hergé kept a collection of newspaper articles and pictures from magazines. We will compare Hergé's drawings with pictures from his archives later on, but first let's look at some drawings that he did just for fun! Look at the first three pages of the story. What do you see? Tintin at the market, of course! But try looking a little closer…

Snowy is scratching himself! How many more times can you see him doing this? Why did Hergé draw Snowy like this?

FLEA MARKET

Markets such as the one that Tintin and Snowy are visiting are sometimes called "flea markets." Some people think that this is because:

★ The goods are infected with fleas

★ The buyers and sellers are as busy as fleas

★ The buyers and sellers are infected with fleas!

Hergé drew Snowy scratching himself as a little joke!

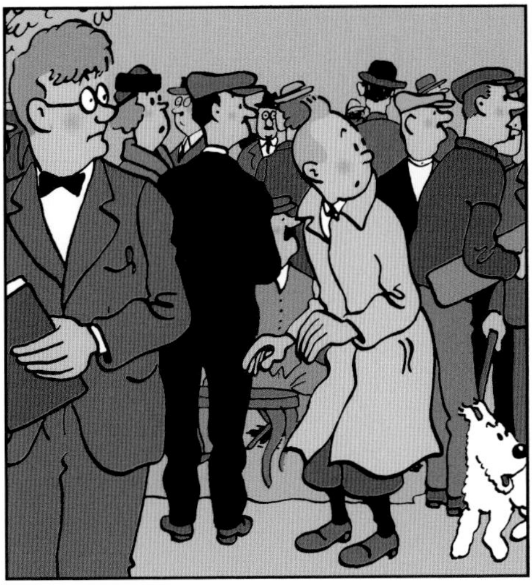

But there is another secret detail on page 2. If you look at the middle frame in the strip at the bottom of the page, you will see a man standing with a book in his hands. This is one of Hergé's real friends and work colleagues, a man named Jacques van Melkebeke!

Hergé sometimes liked to draw his friends into his comic strips.

One more detail

Below, you can see a picture from page 8 in the original French. The arrow shows you that the book that is on Mr. Sakharine's table is entitled *L'Art et la Mer*. This is a real book that Hergé read to find out information before writing his story!

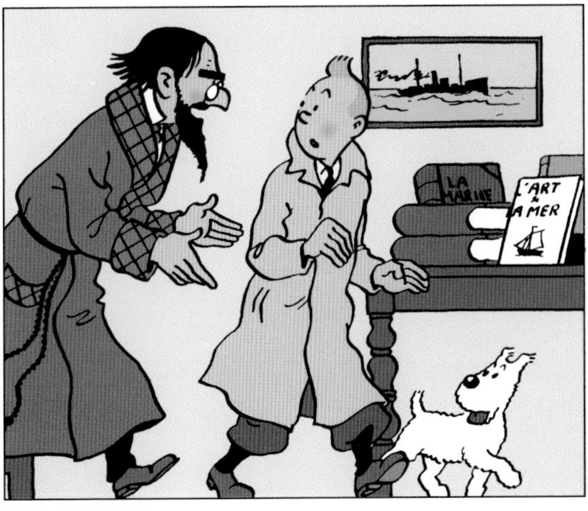

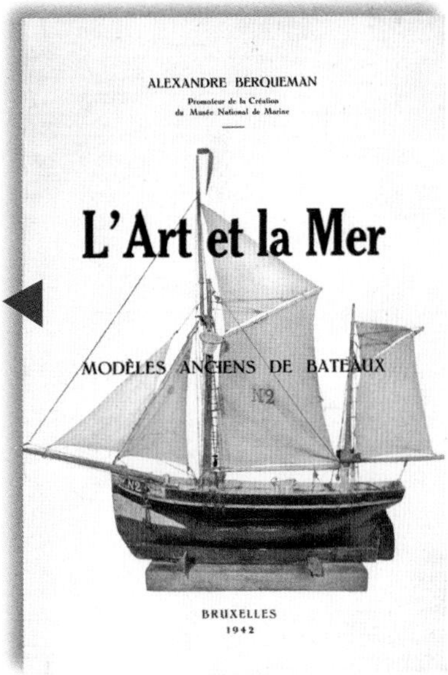
ALEXANDRE BERQUEMAN
Promoteur de la Création
du Musée National de Marine
L'Art et la Mer
MODÈLES ANCIENS DE BATEAUX
BRUXELLES
1942

Now let's look at the magnificent centerpiece of the story, the *Unicorn*.

THE *UNICORN*

Hergé sought expert assistance as he came up with the design for the *Unicorn*. A specialist in model making, Gérard Liger-Belair, drew up the plans for a model of Sir Francis Haddock's ship, which can be seen below. *La Licorne* means *Unicorn* in French!

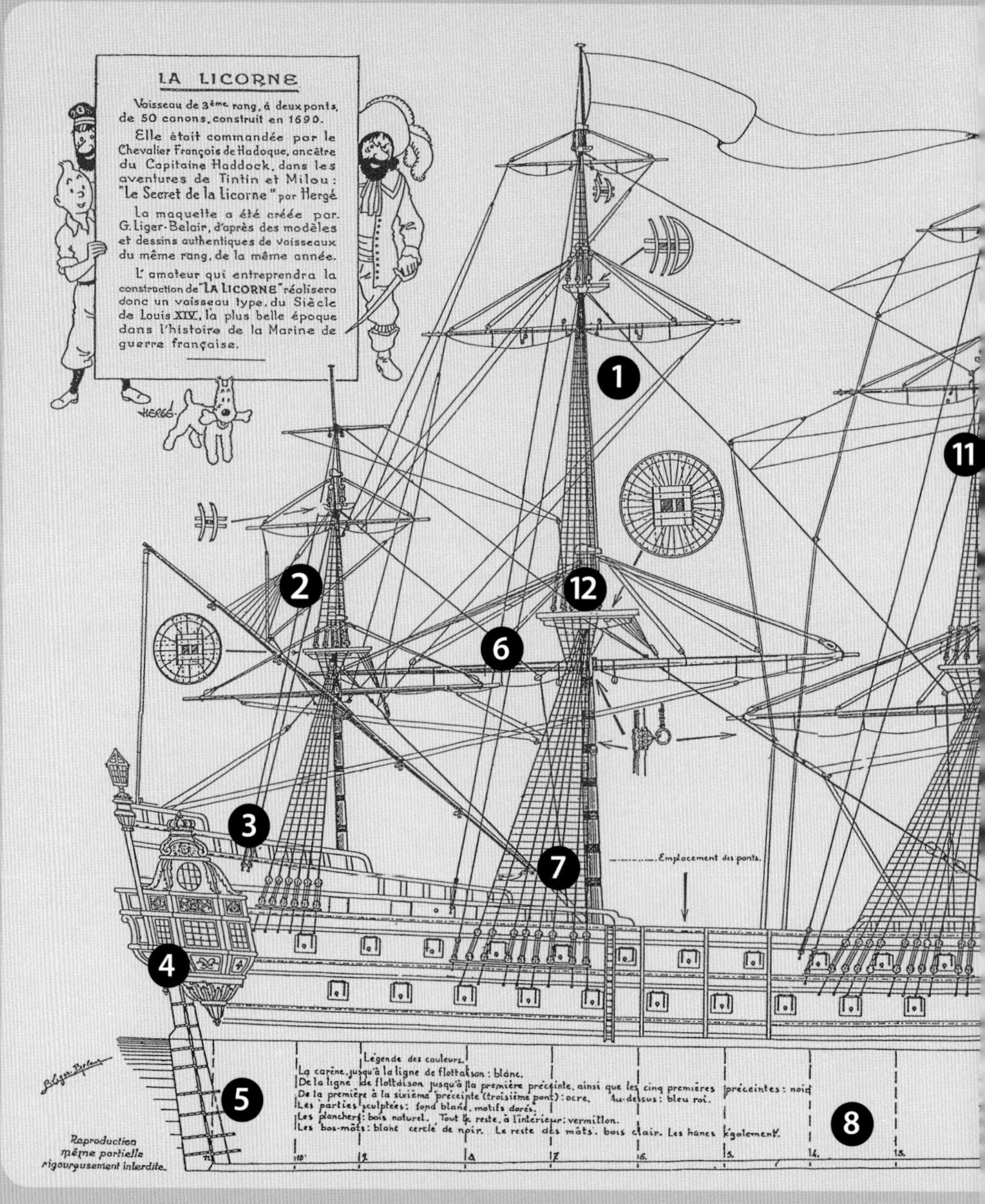

LA LICORNE
Voisseau de 3ème rang, à deux ponts, de 50 canons, construit en 1690.
Elle étoit commandée por le Chevalier François de Hadoque, ancêtre du Capitaine Haddock, dans les aventures de Tintin et Milou : "Le Secret de la Licorne" par Hergé
La maquette a été créée por. G. Liger-Belair, d'après des modèles et dessins authentiques de voisseaux du même rang, de la même année.
L'amateur qui entreprendra la construction de "LA LICORNE" réolisera donc un voisseau type, du Siècle de Louis XIV, la plus belle époque dans l'histoire de la Marine de guerre française.
HERGÉ
1
2
3
4
5
6
7
8
11
12
Emplacement des ponts.
Légende des couleurs.
La carène, jusqu'à la ligne de flottaison : blanc.
De la ligne de flottaison jusqu'à la première précinte, ainsi que les cinq premières préceintes : noir
De la première à la sixième préceinte (troisième pont) : ocre. Au-dessus : bleu roi.
Les parties sculptées : fond blanc, motifs dorés.
Les planchers : bois naturel. Tout le reste, à l'intérieur : vermillon.
Les bas-mâts : blanc cerclé de noir. Le reste des mâts : bois clair. Les hunes également.
Reproduction même partielle rigoureusement interdite.

1 Main-mast	5 Rudder	9 Bowsprit
2 Mizzen-mast	6 Yard	10 Cannons
3 Poop deck	7 Rigging	11 Fore-mast
4 Cabins for captain and important crew	8 Keel	12 Crow's nest

Tous droits réservés à
Gérard LIGER-BELAIR.
Licence 53.T.B.F. Bruxelles.

SHIPS IN THE SEVENTEENTH CENTURY

Based on its size and number of cannons, the *Unicorn* would have been a "third rank" warship. A "first rank" ship such as the real-life *Soleil Royal* (launched in 1670 and from which Hergé copied rigging details), had at least twice as many cannons as a third rank ship, but could carry up to four times as many men!

Soleil Royal

Hergé also used a warship called the *Brillant* (launched in 1690) as a model, but while the *Brillant* had 56 cannons, the *Unicorn* only has 50. Why do you think Hergé gave his ship fewer cannons?

In reality, Red Rackham's small ship would have stood little chance against the larger, better-armed *Unicorn*, so while Hergé copied details from the *Brillant* he removed some cannons to give the pirates a better chance!

DAILY LIFE AS A SAILOR IN THE 1600s

- ★ Any sailor caught messing around could expect lashes from the fearsome whip: the cat o' nine tails.
- ★ No fresh food or water. Sailors ate hard biscuits and drank "grog": 4 parts water + 1 part rum.
- ★ No fresh fruit = no vitamin C. Sailors often caught scurvy, a disease that made their teeth fall out!

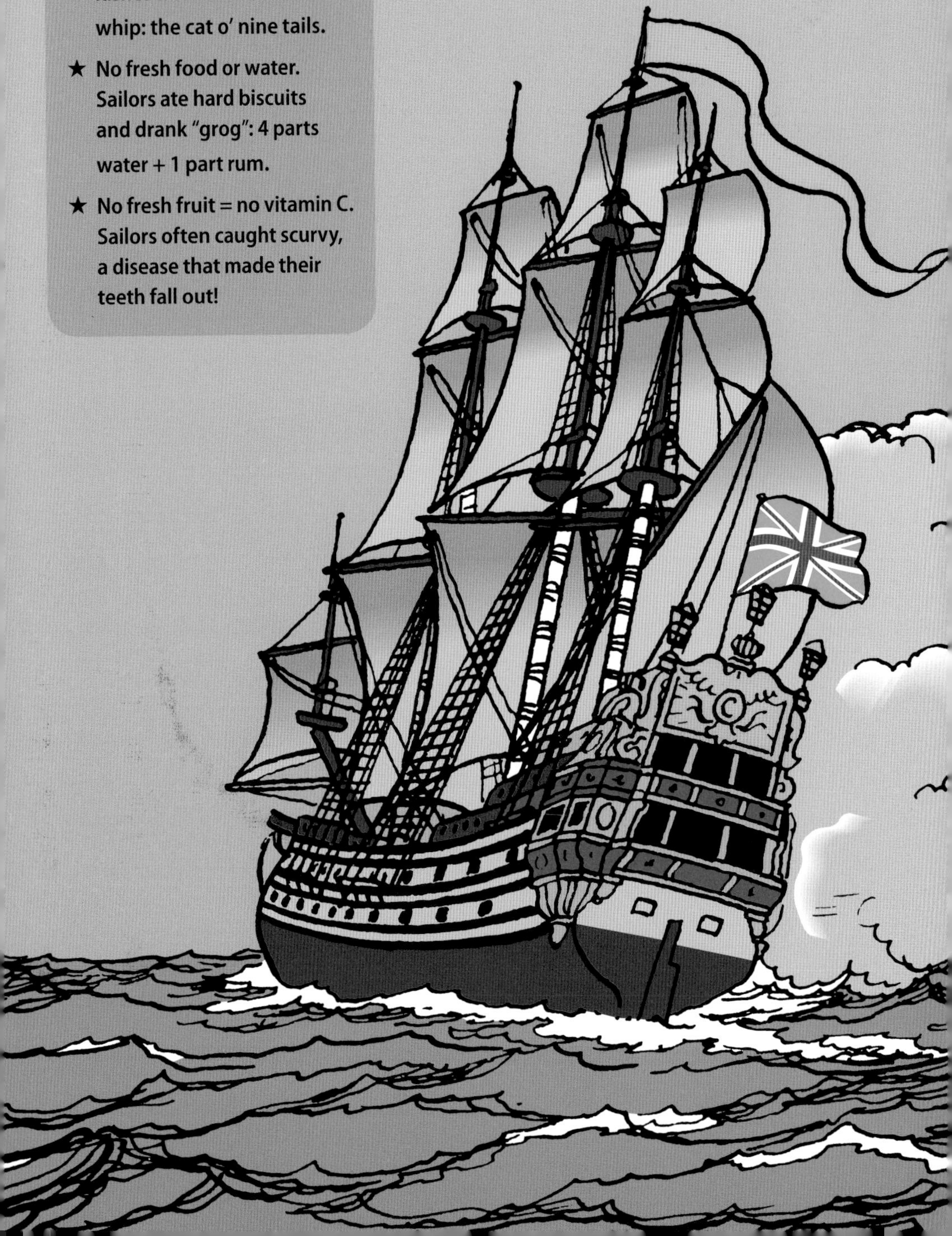

ALL HANDS ON DECK!

Hergé kept pictures of real weapons and clothes in his archives, so that he could draw spectacular scenes extremely accurately. Have a look at the amazing detail in the scene below, compared with the historically accurate weapons and costumes in the painting on the right!

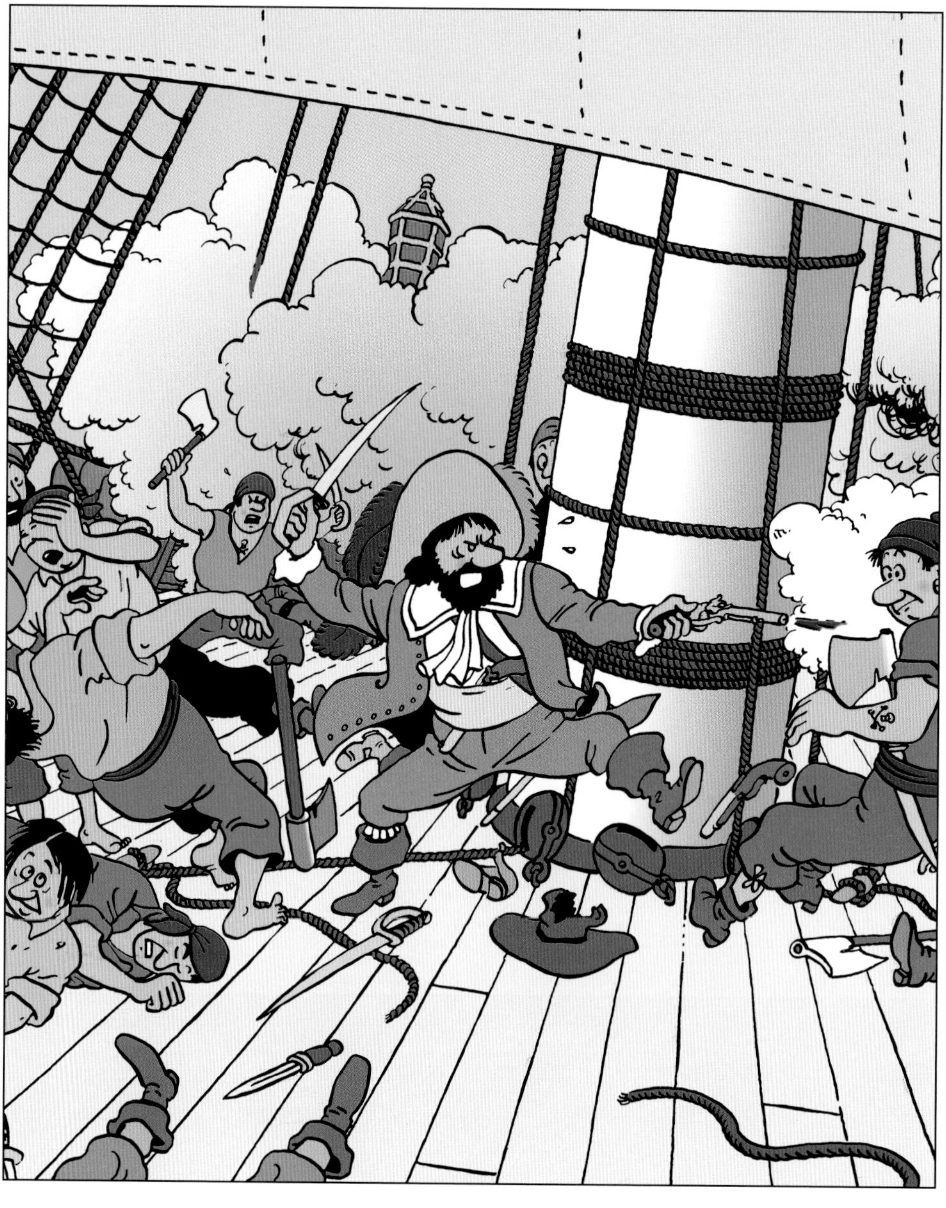

THE PIRATES ATTACK!

Sir Francis Haddock fights valiantly to save his ship and crew. The picture is similar to this painting showing the last battle of fearsome pirate Blackbeard, on November 22, 1718. The pirate lost to Lieutenant Robert Maynard of the British Royal Navy, but he didn't give up without a fight: in the end Blackbeard was shot five times and had twenty cutlass wounds on his body!

BLACKBEARD FACTS

- ★ Blackbeard was an Englishman named Edward Teach.
- ★ The pirate was always armed, with three sets of loaded pistols, two cutlasses and several daggers.
- ★ To make himself appear more terrifying in battle, Blackbeard lit fuses tied into his beard and hair. Don't try this at home!
- ★ In his last fight, Blackbeard shouted "Well done, lad!" when a British soldier wounded him.

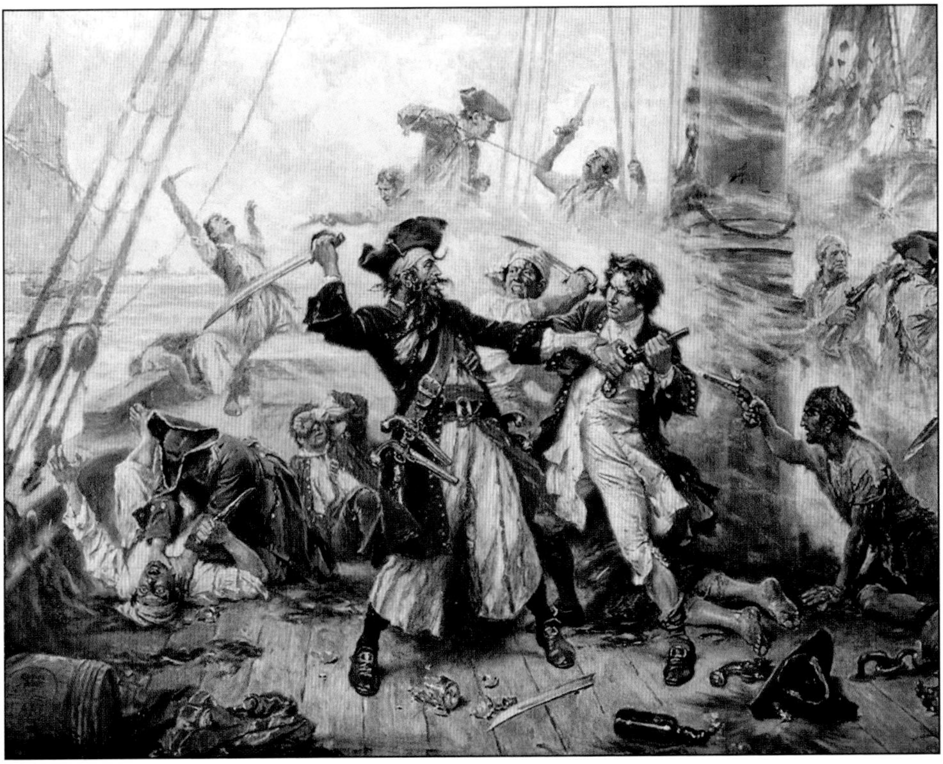

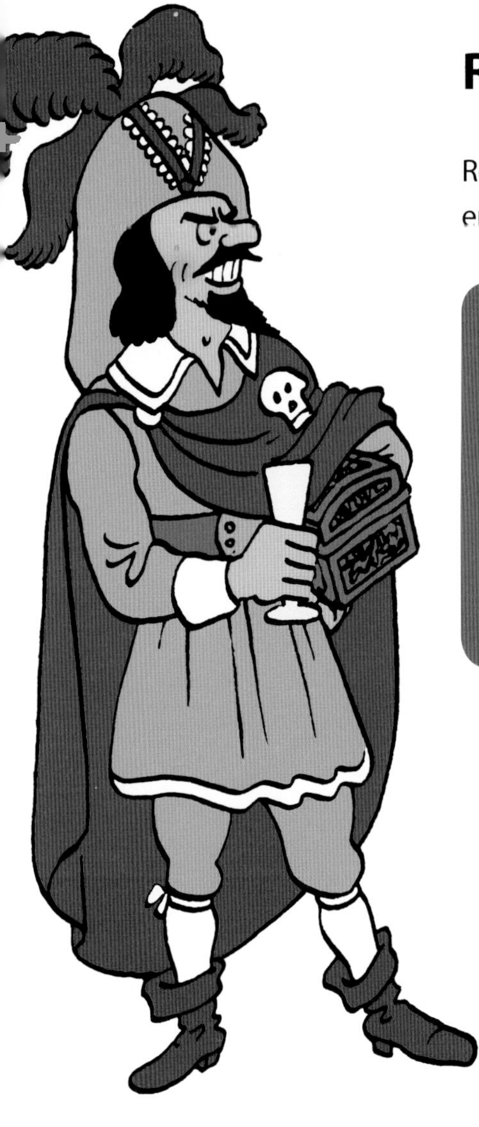

RED RACKHAM

Red Rackham is a fearsome pirate and the enemy of Sir Francis Haddock.

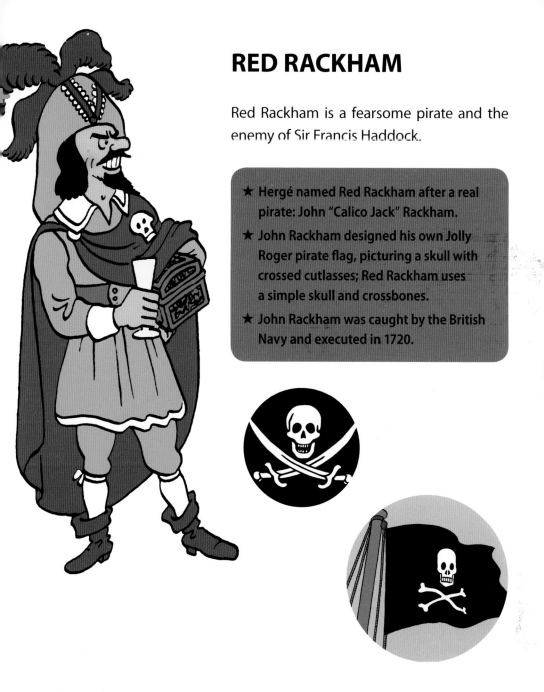

- ★ Hergé named Red Rackham after a real pirate: John "Calico Jack" Rackham.
- ★ John Rackham designed his own Jolly Roger pirate flag, picturing a skull with crossed cutlasses; Red Rackham uses a simple skull and crossbones.
- ★ John Rackham was caught by the British Navy and executed in 1720.

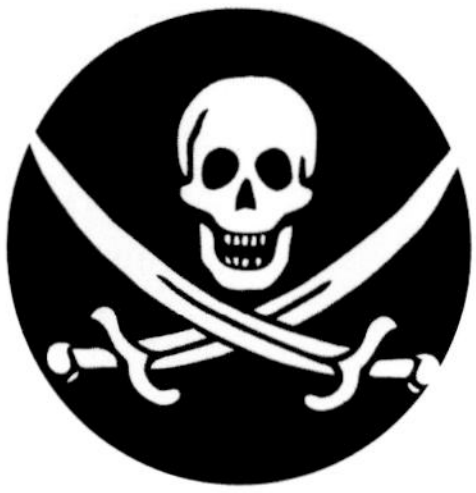

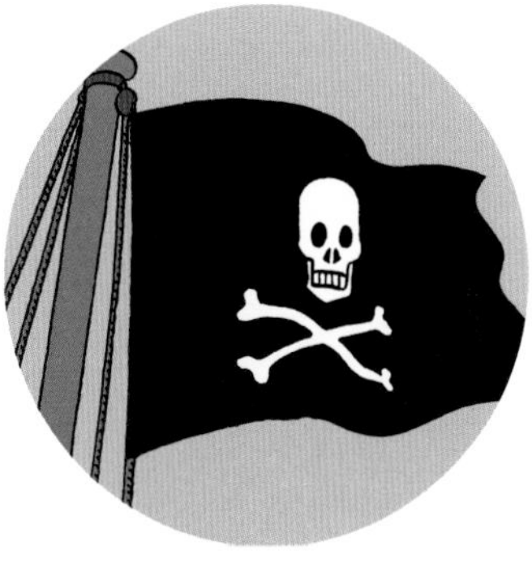

As for Red Rackham, he also meets a violent end, at the end of Sir Francis' sword. Although we only see him in two sequences, Red Rackham makes a big impression. Like all true pirates he is a showman, ruthless and obsessed with treasure. The pirate's notoriety lives on: his name is even used for the title of the next adventure!

SIR FRANCIS HADDOCK

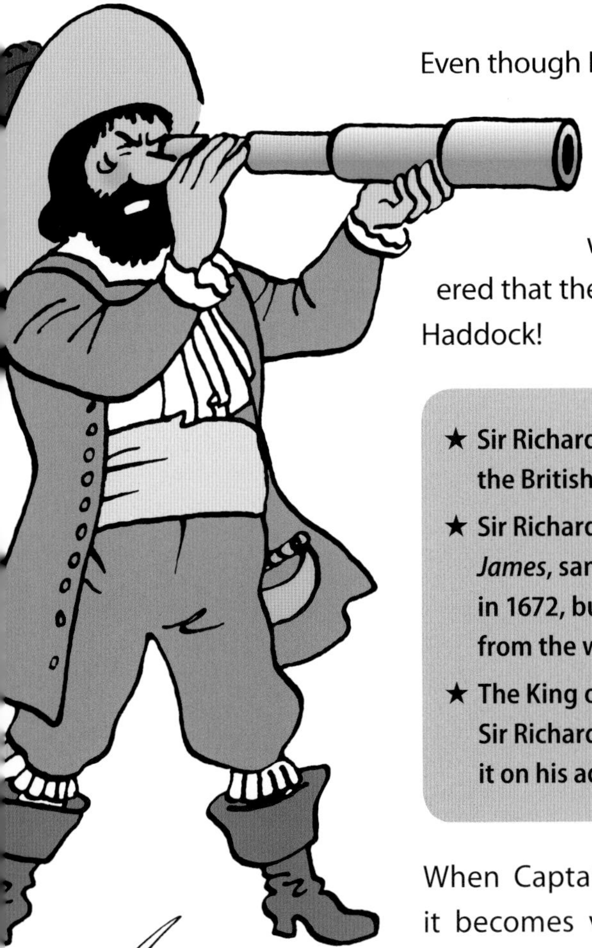

Even though Hergé did not base Sir Francis on a real person, he wrote such realistic stories that often reality caught up with him. After writing this story Hergé discovered that there had once lived a real Admiral Haddock!

- ★ **Sir Richard Haddock was an admiral in the British Navy who lived in the 1600s.**
- ★ **Sir Richard Haddock's ship, the *Royal James*, sank at the Battle of Sole Bay in 1672, but Haddock was pulled from the water alive.**
- ★ **The King of England, Charles II, honored Sir Richard by taking off his hat and placing it on his admiral's head!**

When Captain Haddock gets carried away it becomes very difficult to tell him apart from his ancestor. Fighting blood runs in the family veins!

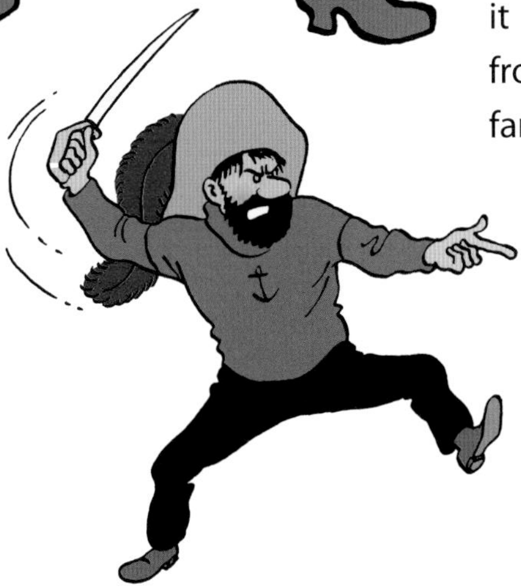

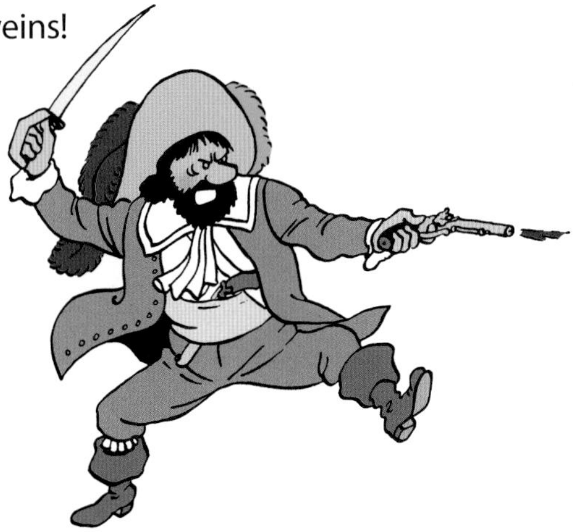

BACK TO THE 1940s

Not long after Captain Haddock has finished his story about his ancestor, we see the first car in the adventure. The car is based on a real vehicle, the 1938 Ford V8. Check out the similarities below between Max Bird's car and the photo of a Ford V8 from Hergé's archives.

La Revue Ford 1938

MARLINSPIKE HALL

In the final part of the story, Tintin is kept prisoner in a large building that we discover is called Marlinspike Hall. In the next Tintin adventure, *Red Rackham's Treasure*, there is another surprise when... well, we won't spoil it for those of you who don't know!

Compare the drawing below with the photo next to it. Hergé's Marlinspike Hall basement is inspired by aspects of several real buildings. He visited the monastery of Saint André in a town called Bruges, as well as Aulne Abbey near Mons, Belgium. Along with the photo below of the crypt at Saint Peter's Church in Brussels, these buildings helped Hergé create the vaulted cellars in Marlinspike Hall.

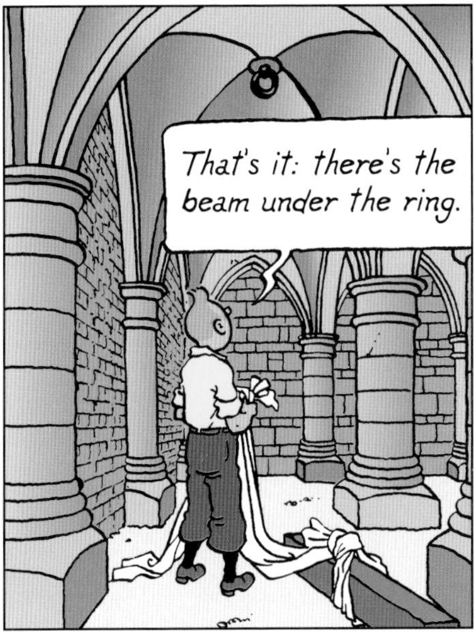
That's it: there's the beam under the ring.

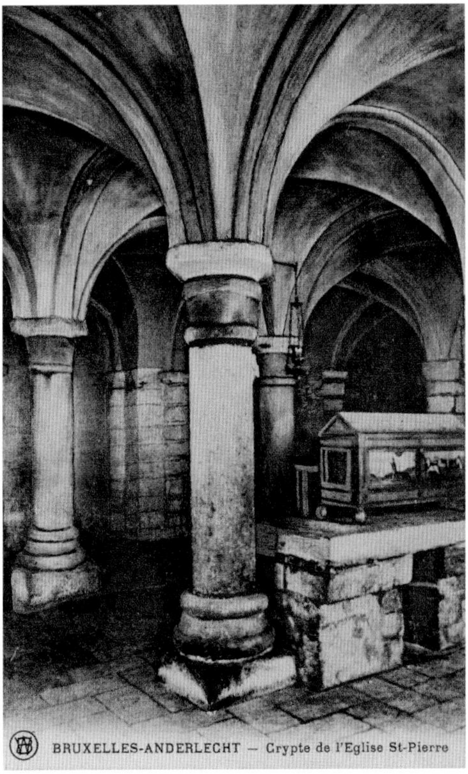
BRUXELLES-ANDERLECHT — Crypte de l'Eglise St-Pierre

CATCH HIM!

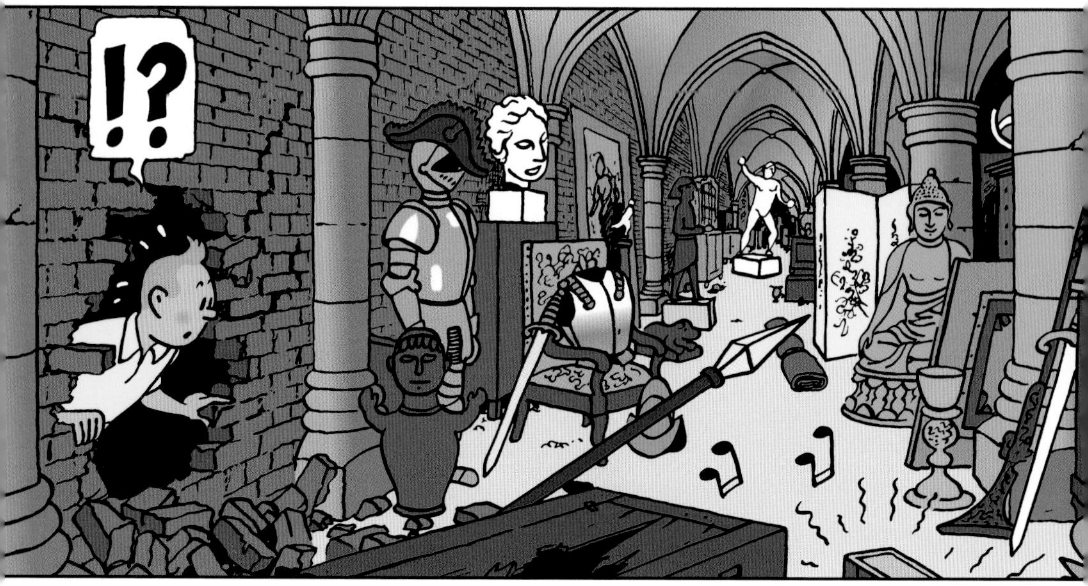
!?

Clever Tintin escapes! The staircase he discovers is based on the inside of a real French mansion: le Château de Cheverny. Look at the photo below.

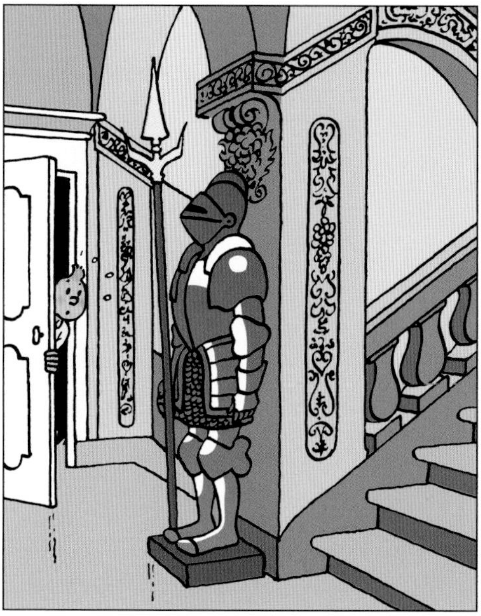

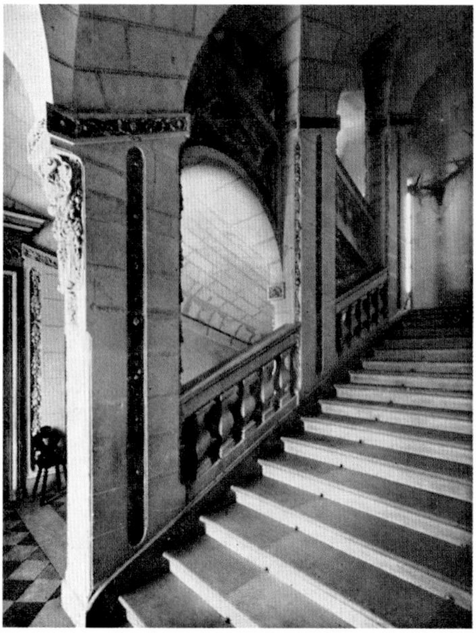

TINTIN'S GRAND ADVENTURE

This story took Hergé in a new direction as he focused on adventure and fantasy. It was the first time that the author worked out carefully how to write an adventure in two parts. The second part of this story (the sequel) is called *Red Rackham's Treasure*. Check it out!

Trivia: *The Secret of the Unicorn*

Hergé knew an old antiques dealer in Brussels who had a private maritime museum. This man's two sons (ex-circus performers) provided Hergé with the inspiration for the Bird brothers.

The Secret of the Unicorn *was Hergé's favorite Tintin adventure until he wrote* Tintin in Tibet.

The title of this adventure is also the title of the first Steven Spielberg Tintin movie: Hergé thought that Steven Spielberg was the only director who could make a good film about Tintin.

- HERGÉ -
LES AVENTURES DE TINTIN
LE SECRET de LA LICORNE
CASTERMAN

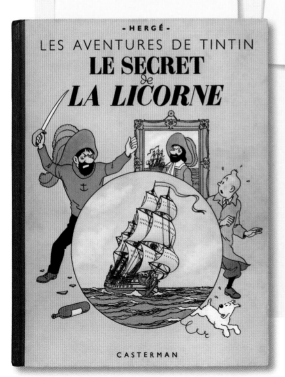

The original cover for *The Secret of the Unicorn* (1943)

GO ON MORE ADVENTURES WITH TINTIN!

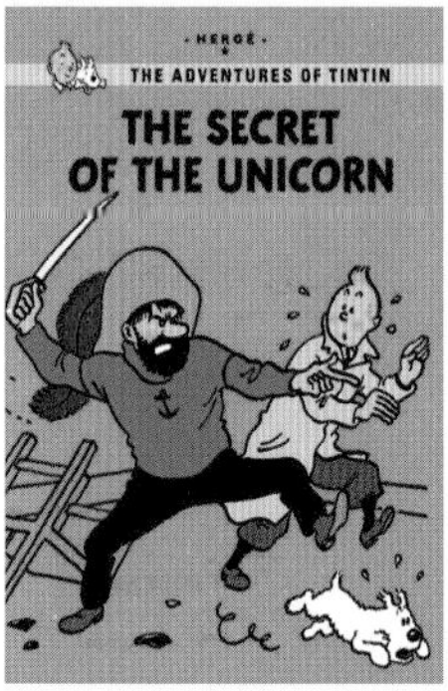
HERGÉ
THE ADVENTURES OF TINTIN
THE SECRET OF THE UNICORN

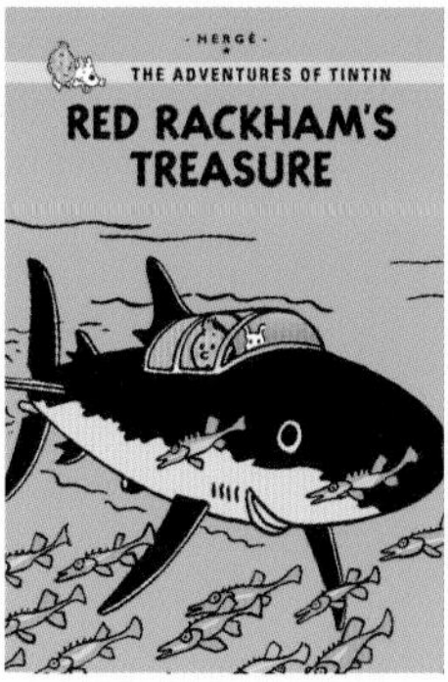
HERGÉ
THE ADVENTURES OF TINTIN
RED RACKHAM'S TREASURE

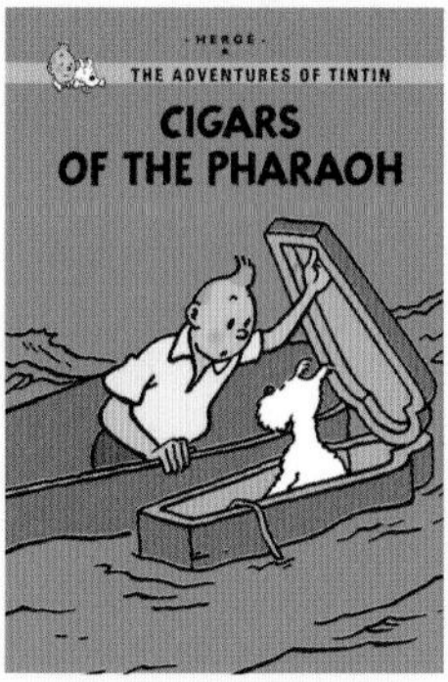
HERGÉ
THE ADVENTURES OF TINTIN
CIGARS OF THE PHARAOH

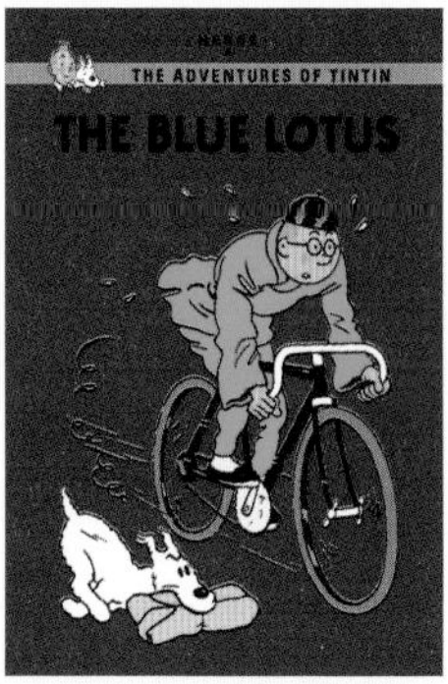
HERGÉ
THE ADVENTURES OF TINTIN
THE BLUE LOTUS

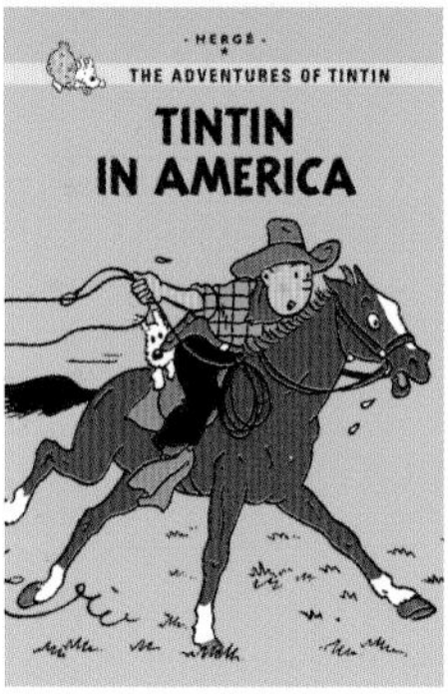
HERGÉ
THE ADVENTURES OF TINTIN
TINTIN IN AMERICA

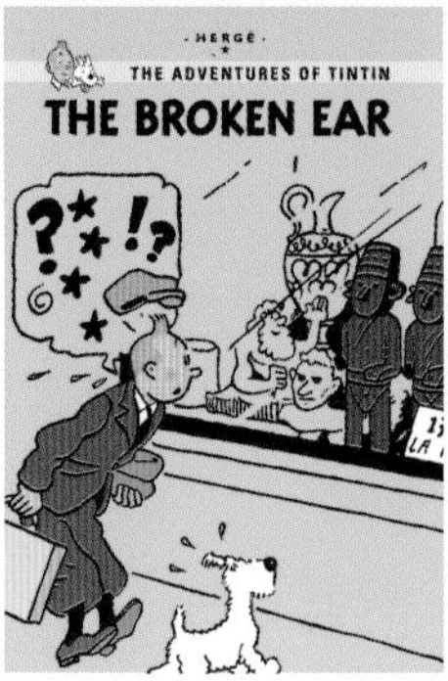
HERGÉ
THE ADVENTURES OF TINTIN
THE BROKEN EAR

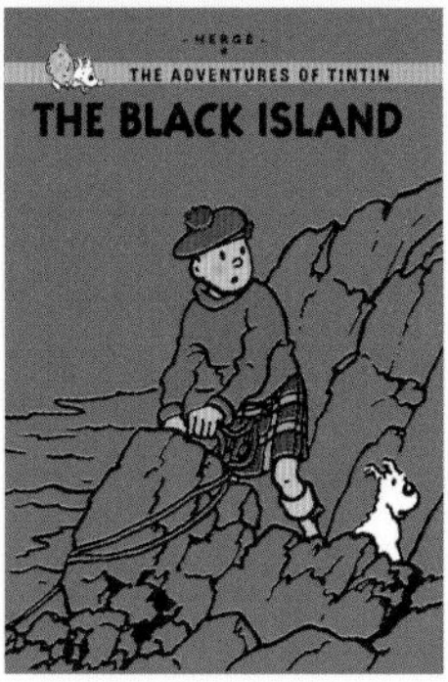
HERGÉ
THE ADVENTURES OF TINTIN
THE BLACK ISLAND

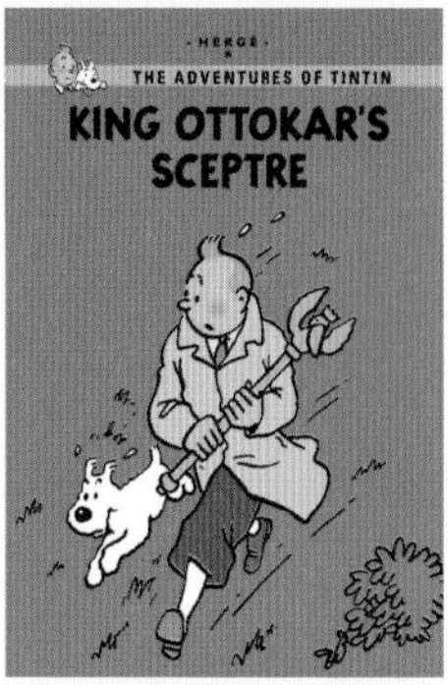
HERGÉ
THE ADVENTURES OF TINTIN
KING OTTOKAR'S SCEPTRE

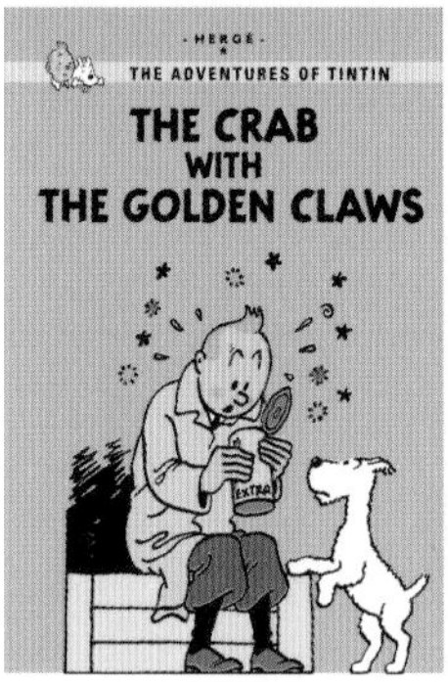
HERGÉ
THE ADVENTURES OF TINTIN
THE CRAB WITH THE GOLDEN CLAWS

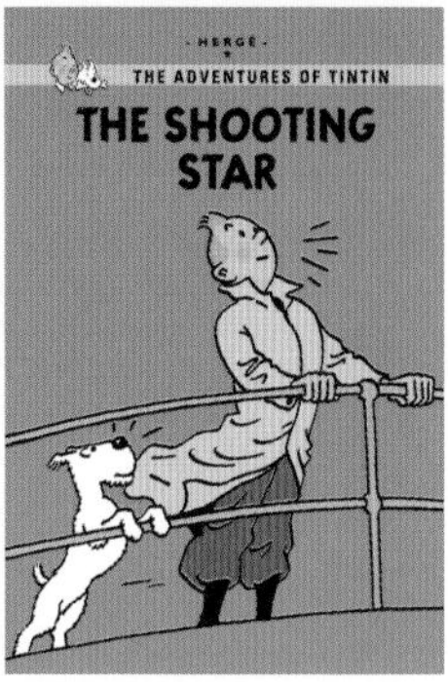
HERGÉ
THE ADVENTURES OF TINTIN
THE SHOOTING STAR

ALSO AVAILABLE

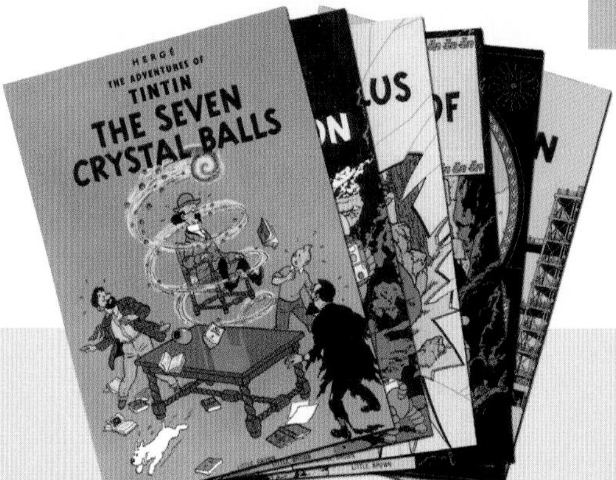
HERGÉ
THE ADVENTURES OF
TINTIN
THE SEVEN CRYSTAL BALLS

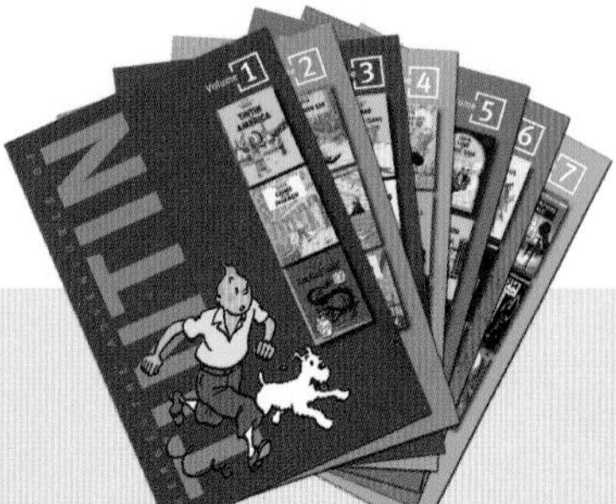
1
2
3
4
5
6
7